TRIBAL
WARFARE

The rifle fire from the Tribesmen began to die away. Blade heard scrabbling noises and hoped they were retreating. The battle noise continued, but now from farther away. It sounded as if the Tribesmen had attacked simultaneously all around the estate, hoping to overwhelm the defenders by surprise and sheer weight of numbers. Now that the defense was rallying, they were moving their new attack to where the first rush had found weak spots. That was better tactics than Blade had ever heard of the Tribesmen using. Either they'd found a war chief who knew modern warfare, or they were getting leadership as well as weaponry from Doimar. Neither was a very pleasant idea.

D1559988

THE BLADE SERIES:

#1 THE BRONZE AXE
#2 THE JADE WARRIOR
#3 JEWEL OF THARN
#4 SLAVE OF SARMA
#5 LIBERATOR OF JEDD
#6 MONSTER OF THE MAZE
#7 PEARL OF PATMOS
#8 UNDYING WORLD
#9 KINGDOM OF ROYTH
#10 ICE DRAGON
#11 DIMENSION OF DREAMS
#12 KING OF ZUNGA
#13 THE GOLDEN STEED
#14 THE TEMPLES OF AYOCAN
#15 THE TOWERS OF MELNON
#16 THE CRYSTAL SEAS
#17 THE MOUNTAINS OF BREGA
#18 WARLORDS OF GAIKON
#19 LOOTERS OF THARN
#20 GUARDIANS OF THE CORAL THRONE
#21 CHAMPION OF THE GODS
#22 THE FORESTS OF GLEOR
#23 EMPIRE OF BLOOD
#24 THE DRAGONS OF ENGLOR
#25 THE TORIAN PEARLS
#26 CITY OF THE LIVING DEAD
#27 MASTER OF THE HASHOMI
#28 WIZARD OF RENTORO
#29 TREASURE OF THE STARS
#30 DIMENSION OF HORROR
#31 GLADIATORS OF HAPANU
#32 PIRATES OF GOHAR
#33 KILLER PLANTS OF BINAARK
#34 THE RUINS OF KALDAK
#35 THE LORDS OF THE CRIMSON RIVER
#36 RETURN TO KALDAK

ATTENTION: SCHOOLS AND CORPORATIONS

PINNACLE Books are available at quantity discounts with bulk purchases for educational, business or special promotional use. For further details, please write to: SPECIAL SALES MANAGER, Pinnacle Books, Inc., 1430 Broadway, New York, NY 10018.

WRITE FOR OUR FREE CATALOG

If there is a Pinnacle Book you want—and you cannot find it locally—it is available from us simply by sending the title and price plus 75¢ to cover mailing and handling costs to:

Pinnacle Books, Inc.
Reader Service Department
1430 Broadway
New York, NY 10018

Please allow 6 weeks for delivery.

_____Check here if you want to receive our catalog regularly.

BLADE

RETURN TO KALDAK
Jeffrey Lord

TM

Created by the producers of
The Windhaven Saga, Wagons West, and
The Kent Family Chronicles Series.

Executive Producer: Lyle Kenyon Engel

PINNACLE BOOKS **NEW YORK**

This is a work of fiction. All the characters and events portrayed in this book are fictional, and any resemblance to real people or incidents is purely coincidental.

BLADE #36: RETURN TO KALDAK

Copyright © 1983 by Book Creations, Inc.

All rights reserved, including the right to reproduce this book or portions thereof in any form.

An original Pinnacle Books edition, published for the first time anywhere.

Produced by Book Creations, Inc. Lyle Kenyon Engel executive producer.

First printing, March 1983

ISBN: 523-41210-X

Cover illustration by Kevin Johnson

Printed in the United States of America

PINNACLE BOOKS, INC.
1430 Broadway
New York, New York 10018

RETURN
TO KALDAK

Chapter 1

The dark green Rover pulled into a reserved space in the parking lot. The man who got out wore a tweed sport jacket, corduroy trousers, and nondescript walking shoes. The clothing didn't disguise his powerful frame or his athlete's grace of movement as he walked toward one of the brick buildings around the parking lot.

He was hatless, so the breeze ruffled thick black hair cut unfashionably short. Women were apt to describe his face as ruggedly handsome. This did no justice to the penetrating quality of his large gray eyes. They flicked their gaze continuously from point to point, never leaving anything around him unobserved for more than a few seconds.

Then the man reached the door of the building and vanished from the sight of the two men watching from the window above. The taller one turned to the other and said, "As much as I hate to admit it, Richard looks in splendid form."

"You don't really hate to admit that he's fit for another trip, do you, J?" said the second man.

"Not really, Leighton. But if I thought he weren't, I'd insist on a delay no matter what hopes you had for your new booth!"

Leighton ran his long arthritic fingers through what remained of his white hair. Then he smiled thinly. "I hardly need to be reminded of that, J."

"True." Lord Leighton was actually being exceptionally moderate. His scientific genius was world famous. So was his temper. When someone seemed to be in the way of one of his experiments, he behaved like a she-bear defending her cubs. Although he was past eighty, he showed no signs of mellowing.

But then, J reflected, that was hardly to be expected. The man *was* a bloody genius, and had a right to be proud of it, particularly when he was still producing fine work. Also, if you're born with a hunchback and half-crippled by polio as a child, you learn to fight your own battles early. No one else will fight them for you. Not for the first time, J thanked whatever or whoever was responsible that he himself still enjoyed good health at an age when he could have been drawing his civil service pension.

The main reason J wasn't retired was the man who'd just entered the building. His name was Richard Blade. J had picked him as a promising candidate for the secret intelligence agency MI6A when Blade was fresh out of Oxford. He'd more than fulfilled that promise.

Then Lord Leighton conceived the experiment of linking an advanced computer with a human brain—Blade's, to be precise. He hoped to create a superior combination of human and electronic intelligence, by having the computer generate a field matching Blade's brain waves. The actual result was Blade's being hurled off into a parallel world. Leighton christened it Dimension X after Blade got back.

Giving the mystery world a name didn't make it any the less mysterious. It didn't help, either, that Blade turned out to be the only man in the free world who could make the journey. Others returned insane or not at all. Millions of pounds and dozens of Lord Leighton's experiments later, this was still true. Meanwhile, J had a busy time defending Project Dimension X from enemy agents, accidents, and sheer human stupidity. He had almost as busy a time defending Richard Blade from Leighton's wilder experiments.

2

To J, BLade was more than a friend or a trusted subordinate. He was the son the aging bachelor spymaster would never have. To Leighton, Blade was hardly more than an experimental guinea pig.

Or at least he *had* been once. That was before Leighton's experiment with the new KALI computer let an immaterial but deadly monster from another Dimension loose on the world. Blade eventually defeated the Ngaa, and Leighton seemed to have learned his lesson. At least he hadn't sprung either of his latest ideas on J and Blade at the last minute, the way he used to.

Also, the Project was actually beginning to creep toward solutions to some of its long-standing problems. Blade could now take some equipment with him, even though it had to be expensively fabricated from a special alloy he'd discovered in a Dimension called Englor. The transitions themselves no longer left him weakened or suffering from headaches. From the last trip he'd even brought back a live, functional animal—

"Yeep!" A small brightly colored shape darted out from behind Lord Leighton's desk. It was Cheeky, the "Feathered One" from the Dimension of the Crimson River. He was about the size and shape of a monkey, but covered from head to foot with bright blue and green feathers instead of fur.

He was also telepathic.

J had always been open-minded about the possibility of telepathy. He'd seen too many odd things in too many lands only a little less strange than Dimension X. Leighton had always been a militant skeptic.

What Cheeky did when he was around Blade had converted J to a believer. Even Leighton was saying, "I'd like to run some experiments under carefully controlled conditions. That's been the biggest stumbling block in dealing with ESP—poorly designed experiments run by believers or outright nut cases!"

J put his foot down, however, on running the experiments right after Blade's return from the Dimension of the Crimson River. Blade was obviously suffering from something like combat fatigue. Although he was the sanest and toughest man J had ever known, with enough courage and survival skills for any six normal people, Blade still reached the limits of endurance at times.

Was the sheer loneliness of Blade's profession also catching up with him? J had to wonder. Blade's fiance, Zoe Cornwall, had broken off her engagement because the Official Secrets Act didn't let him explain his trips to Dimension X. When they were on the verge of getting back together, she was kidnapped and horribly killed by the Ngaa. By all accounts Blade had left a good dozen children in the various lands of Dimension X, but in England he had neither wife nor child nor steady girlfriend nor much of a home life to help him forget the grim battles he had to fight alone in Dimension X.

That was why J was so glad when Blade went out and bought himself a country house in Hampshire. He was even happier to hear that Lord Leighton contributed part of the money. Now Richard was busily restoring the place. While he was doing this, he'd be too busy between trips to feel lonely. When the house was finished, he would have a place he could call his own to come back to.

If he lived long enough, he would even be able to retire there and—who could say?—marry and raise a family.

Cheeky *yeeeeped* again, breaking J's train of thought, and started racing around the room. Leighton stood protectively in front of his desk, arms spread wide to keep the feather-monkey from jumping up on it and scattering valuable papers to the four winds. J wondered if it was his own thoughts about Richard Blade which had excited the little animal. Then he heard familiar footsteps on the stairs outside the office.

So did Cheeky. He ran to the door, leaped up, and caught the doorknob with both paws. He swung there, turning the knob while he kicked at the door frame with both feet. The door swung open and Richard Blade walked in.

Seen close up, he seemed to have gone gray-haired all at once. Then J took a still closer look and recognized plaster dust. He also saw dark rings of grit under Blade's usually well-manicured fingernails.

"Just come from the house, Richard?"

"Drove up this morning," said Blade with a grin. "The workers knocked off at their usual time, leaving the job half-arsed. So I finished it off myself. Up until midnight doing it, too, and then of course there wasn't any hot water!"

Leighton made a tut-tutting noise of mock indignation. "The union will get you for that, Richard."

"What they don't know won't hurt them," said Blade cheerfully. "Besides, the contractor's foreman is the son of my father's old groom. *He's* not going to sneak."

"Good," said J. 'How is the house coming, by the way?" He'd seen it once. It was an eighteenth-century squire's establishment, appallingly run-down when Blade acquired it.

"Well, we can keep partridges and stray pigs out of the ground-floor rooms now. There are four rooms on the upper floor where you don't need an umbrella when it rains. And you can light at least one fireplace without fumigating the whole house."

At this point Cheeky *yeeeped* indignantly at being ignored and took a flying leap onto Blade's shoulder. Blade scratched his feathery crest absentmindedly, without taking his eyes off Lord Leighton and J.

"Well, from the look on His Lordship's face I should say he's pickled another bright idea for us," he said. "Do I go through hanging from a trapeze this time?"

J swallowed his laughter. Leighton merely shook his head. "No. It's simply a couple of logical extrapolations from our experience last time."

The last trip into Dimension X, Leighton used a

5

new technique. Whereas in the past Blade had been greased up and wired all over with electrodes, for the last trip he had stood in the middle of a booth of wire mesh, charged with an electrical field linked to the computer. Since he always came back without being physically linked to the computer, why couldn't he go the same way?

It worked—once. Leighton had a scientist's confidence that what had worked once would work again, under the same conditions. J was less optimistic, but he was willing to go along with the scientist, if Richard agreed.

Leighton explained. "With the new booth, there is a lot more room within the area the electrical field covers. Room for more than a more-or-less naked Blade. We don't have a second person trained and ready to go, but we do have Cheeky."

Blade's first mental reaction must have been negative. Cheeky stood up, *yeeeping* indignantly, his feathers bristling, shaking both paws at Lord Leighton. "Easy, Cheeky, easy," said Blade.

Leighton went on. "Cheeky is particularly suitable because of his small size, and his association with Blade." (J noted that Leighton didn't use the word "telepathy.") "He is also intelligent enough to survive for a while if he and Blade got separated."

"A short while, yes," said Blade dubiously. "But that depends on the climate and the weather. I'll have to ask him." Leighton's eyebrows rose, and Blade's voice hardened. "If you treat him as an experimental animal with no will of his own, I won't take him. I won't even leave him in your hands while I'm gone, and the devil take the Official Secrets Act!"

J nodded. He rather wished Richard hadn't forced the issue so bluntly, but he certainly had the right of it.

"Very well," said Leighton. "You can ask his consent. But before you do, let me finish, *if* you please."

"The worst danger, Leighton continued, "is in the

6

transitions into Dimension X and back to Home Dimension. You see, we're not sure exactly how much molecular cohesion a body retains while transitioning between Dimensions. You've done your best to describe your sensations, Blade, but I'm afraid it hasn't been good enough."

J relaxed. If Leighton was willing to admit any sort of limits on their knowledge of the experiment, he was likely to be reasonable. Then the scientist's next words grabbed his attention.

"If your molecules and Cheeky's lose their cohesion on the way, they might intermingle. They might also not—ah—sort themselves out before you reached the other side. Do you remember the film *The Fly*?"

Blade obviously did. So did J. He imagined a monstrous creature, half Blade and half Cheeky, stumbling out of the booth or lost in the wilderness of some unknown Dimension. Only a lifetime of self-control kept Blade's nausea from showing on his face.

"If the new booth hadn't worked out so smoothly the first time, I'd have my doubts," said Blade slowly. "As it is, I'm willing to try it. What about you, Cheeky?" He spoke as if he was speaking to an intelligent, rational being. J found himself looking around for the person being addressed.

"Yik-yik-yeeeek!" went the feather-monkey. Then he hopped up on top of Blade's head and clung with all his fingers and toes buried in Blade's hair. Blade stood with a long-suffering expression until Cheeky climbed back down onto his shoulder. Then he nodded.

"He's willing to try it."

"Splendid!" said Leighton, with genuine relief and enthusiasm in his voice. "The new booth *is* a real breakthrough. The faster we can exploit it, the faster we can make the Project really successful. Or at least less vulnerable to accidents," he added. "I'll really sleep a trifle better when the Project can survive Richard's falling off a ladder while fixing the roof on that confounded Hampshire mausoleum of his!"

7

"I couldn't agree more," said Blade. "In fact, do we need to limit my equipment anymore? The fabric and rubber material I took through last time survived as well as the Englor Alloy."

"More equipment, as well as Cheeky?" said J dubiously. "That's two experiments on one trip."

"True," said Blade. "But some sort of backpacking outfit shouldn't make that much difference. I was also thinking of Cheeky. I can forage for my meals or tighten my belt better than he can. I've got to take some food for him, at least." The feather-monkey *yeeeped* in apparent approval.

"I must say I was thinking along similar lines myself," said Leighton. "I would suggest some care, though. We've got a second knife made of EA Two, so you'll have a spare. We can also make up one for Cheeky in a few days. Other than that, I'd suggest not taking anything metal. Above all, no guns. I'd be a trifle uneasy about subjecting anything explosive to the new field this time."

"I wasn't thinking of a gun," said Blade. "It's the sort of thing I might find a bit hard to explain if I landed in a pretechnological society. I've been suspected of black magic often enough as it is. What about one of those knockdown crossbows we used to have in MI6A? You remember them, sir. Fit in an attaché case, but a two-hundred-pound pull and no metal in them."

J nodded. "I think I still have enough influence to rout one of them out of the Weapons people."

"Then it's settled, is it?" said Leighton.

"As far as I'm concerned, it is," said Blade. "What about you, sir?"

J still had reservations. This was going to be the biggest leap into the dark since the original KALI computer. However, they were already far beyond the limits of what anyone outside the Project considered science. What did they have to lose?

"Might as well be hung for a sheep as for a lamb," said J. "See you next week, Richard." They shook

8

hands, and J also reached up and patted Cheeky's head. Blade had tried to teach the feather-monkey to shake hands, but he flatly refused.

Outside, J was so preoccupied as he walked to his car that he was nearly run down by a delivery truck pulling into Complex Two. Several men came out and started unloading crates and film canisters. J watched them idly for a moment. It seemed that Complex Two was growing every time he came.

Well, it certainly didn't hurt the Project to have room to expand. There was already more than enough equipment and people to fill two of the three buildings. If the Project was on the edge of a real breakthrough . . .

J firmly squelched his optimism and climbed into his car. No matter how close they were to a breakthrough, everything still depended on Richard Blade.

Chapter 2

During the next few days, everyone's nerves were stretched tight over the risks they were taking. Blade tried at first to assemble his equipment from many different countries, so that no one would be able to tell where he himself came from. He spent several days trying to find South African hiking boots and Czech canteens before realizing that he was wasting his time. The Russians had penetrated Project Dimension X twice, but both times their agents had died before revealing its secret. It was highly unlikely that he would meet anyone in Dimension X who knew or cared where his gear came from.

He still carefully tore off all the labels and tags. If he landed in an advanced society, someone might notice the strange language and the unknown names and get curious. Such curiosity could be as dangerous to the Dimension X secret as Russian spies, even if it didn't have immediate consequences in Home Dimension.

Blade bought new clothing and equipment, but decided to keep his old hiking boots, which were well broken-in and comfortable. He was prepared to die for England but not get unnecessary blisters for it.

Cheeky was a strict vegetarian, but he would eat nearly anything which wasn't meat. Blade had seen him munch brussels sprouts, daffodil bulbs, and scraps of leather. The same fruits, nuts, whole-grain cereal bars, and chocolate Blade was going to eat would also do for Cheeky.

Lord Leighton was not only nervous but found time on his hands. He kept making telephone calls to both J and Blade, fussing over trifles. The last straw came when he rang up Blade to ask which sedatives should be given to Cheeky when he was sent through the transition.

"No," said Blade, "I won't suggest what sedatives to use! I will not cooperate with this whole idiotic proposal! If you go on with it, you'll never find Cheeky, and you may have some trouble finding me!"

"Richard, you're—"

"I'm not what you're going to say I am, that's for bloody well certain. I'm tired of Cheeky's being treated as an experimental animal, that's what I am!

"Besides," he added. "You're forgetting the telepathic link between me and Cheeky. Sedation might break it. How can we be sure he'll go with me without the telepathy? Can we even be sure of finding a safe sedative without a pile of experiments? Do you want to delay the next trip?"

"If you'd given us a free hand with Cheeky when you came back from the Crimson River, we could have made the experiments by now," said Leighton.

"Well, I didn't. With the attitude you're showing now, I think I was bloody well right!"

After a long silence Leighton cleared his throat. "Richard, I'm sorry I raised the matter. I said I wouldn't put pressure on you. I meant it. I'm afraid I'm not thinking quite as clearly as I ought to. The strain, you know."

That was more of an apology than Leighton ever gave anybody, and Blade decided to accept it, such as it was. "I understand," he said. "Well, let's get me and Cheeky fired off into Dimension X, and you and J can both relax."

*   *   *

Blade still didn't breathe easy until two days later, when he and Cheeky showed up in Complex One ready for the trip into Dimension X. Complex One lay two hundred feet below the Tower of London, with a concealed entrance guarded by dark-suited Special Branch men. Once it held the whole Project, and it still held the master computer, the new booth, and everything else which might give away the secret of Dimension X.

That wasn't enough to fill the whole Complex. An entire corridor of offices and laboratories once alive with lights and voices and hard work was now dark and empty, the equipment having gone to the new Complex Two or else shrouded in dust covers. Blade had the feeling ghosts would be lurking in those empty rooms before long.

As usual, Blade stepped into the changing booth to get ready. Once, had had to strip to a loincloth and smear himself with foul-smelling black grease to prevent electrical burns from the mass of electrodes which linked him to the computer. Now he pulled on net underwear, heavy socks, woolen trousers and shirt, and a light windbreaker. He slipped one knife into a wrist sheath and hung the other along with a canteen on his belt. A light rucksack held a poncho, a spare canteen, extra socks and underwear, soap and toothbrush, several days' rations for himself and Cheeky, water purification tablets, snares, fishing line, and the disassembled crossbow.

Meanwhile, Cheeky was pulling on a modified dog sweater and belting on his own miniature knife. He wasn't quite intelligent enough to reason out for himself how to use unknown tools. He only had to be shown a couple of times, though.

With Cheeky perched on his shoulder, Blade stood as the wire-mesh booth was lowered over him. Last trip it had been about the same size and shape as the glass booth which held the rubber-padded chair of the original computer, before the KALI capsule. For this trip it was six inches larger all around, to provide just enough room for Cheeky. Looking out through the mesh, Blade saw Leighton standing by the manual control panel.

That was all right with Blade. For the first time he wouldn't reach Dimension X alone. For the first time he was also taking someone else into its unknown dangers. He was glad to see that Leighton wasn't adding to those dangers unnecessarily by using the untested new automatic sequencer.

"All right, Richard?" said Leighton.

Blade gave a thumbs-up gesture and Cheeky imitated him. Leighton's hand pulled the red master switch in one swift motion to the bottom of the slot.

From where J sat on a folding stool, the booth suddenly seemed filled with green light, with Blade and Cheeky clearly visible inside it. Then the light turned silvery, Blade and Cheeky blurred, and both they and the light vanished.

Leighton stood with his hand on the switch until the lights on the consoles seemed to satisfy him. To J, they made less sense than so many Egyptian hierogylphics. Finally the scientist turned to J.

"Do you need a drink as badly as I do?"

"Probably more so."

"I sincerely doubt if that would be possible," said Leighton. He reached under the control panel and came out with a silver flask and a thermos jug.

"Weak or strong?"

Blade only saw the green light. Then the wire mesh and the room beyond it wavered. He seemed to be looking at them through the hot air rising from a fire. He felt a stab of some strong emotion in his mind from Cheeky, not quite fear but certainly discontent with the situation.

Easy, Cheeky, thought Blade. *I've been through this dozens of times. It's not so bad after the first time.* He hoped it was nothing more than facing the unknown which was bothering Cheeky.

Then the green light and the wavering booth

and room both vanished. Blade felt Cheeky's weight lift from his shoulder and heard him *yeeep*. He sounded more angry than frightened, but suddenly his thoughts weren't reaching Blade.

Then Blade felt himself falling. He fell down through dreamlike cold and blackness for what seemed like forever. It was so cold that he felt the sweat on his skin starting to freeze, and so black that even the idea of light seemed impossible.

His thoughts still came clearly. He'd just begun to wonder if something might have gone badly wrong, when suddenly the cold and the darkness vanished. There was blue sky overhead, damp grass under his hands, and a cool breeze puffing against his face.

Blade sat up. He was sitting in foot-high grass on a slope which looked like the bank of a river. Between the water's edge and the main channel lay a hundred yards of dead trees, patches of black mud, and clumps of reeds. The reeds were a sickly yellow-green, and looked vaguely familiar.

Behind him the bank rose toward the crest of a hill. The grass gave way to scrubby bushes, and the bushes to gnarled trees. High above the treetops, a large bird made lazy circles with hardly the flicker of a wingtip, riding the updrafts.

There was no sign of Cheeky.

Blade controlled both his fear for Cheeky and his anger at Lord Leighton until he'd finished checking his clothes, his equipment, and the shape of his body. He was intact, and he had everything he'd taken into the booth—except for Cheeky. He waited a minute, for signs of either the feather-monkey or less-welcome company. Then he pulled out his canteen and walked down to the water's edge.

The water of the river was too scummy and dark with decayed vegetable matter for drinking, but a clear stream flowed down the bank a few yards away. Blade drank, filled both canteens and added water purification tablets, then hooked the canteens to his

14

belt. At last he started searching for Cheeky in earnest, using not only his eyes and ears but his mind.

Cheeky, where are you? Cheeky, answer me. Cheeky, are you hurt?

Blade sent his thoughts out over and over again, keeping the message simple. For all the answer he got, he might as well have been trying to explain Einstein's Theory of Relativity.

He didn't see or hear anything, either. He began to wonder if perhaps Cheeky had thought Blade was dead or hurt and gone off in search of help. He went back to where he'd awakened and looked at the grass. It was flattened, but not crushed as if he'd lain there for a long time. Also, if he'd been there long enough to make Cheeky think he was dead, he'd feel chilled and stiff.

No, Cheeky was—lost. Blade would not use the word "gone," let alone the word "dead," even in his mind. Cheeky was lost. The main problem for now was to find him again.

His anger at Lord Leighton slowly passed off. Cheeky had known what he was getting into, as well as his mind could grasp it. He was a volunteer. And certainly the failure of one of his most cherished and promising experiments would be its own punishment for Lord Leighton. He'd be miserably disappointed.

So was Blade. He hadn't realized until now how much he'd hoped that the problem of facing a new world alone was solved. He'd always been a loner, too much so for a safe, sane, twentieth-century existence. But a man can fight only so many single-handed battles before he starts wanting someone to guard his back and share his campfire.

More than his own peace of mind was also involved here. Why send two people into Dimension X if they didn't arrive together? Blade was going to spend several days looking for Cheeky before he started exploring this Dimension. He'd have spent even more time looking for a human companion.

It was frustrating, to put it mildly. Trying to solve

15

several problems at once, they'd wound up solving none of them! They weren't quite back to where they'd started, but they were close enough to make Blade angry.

He let his anger out with a few heartfelt curses. The outburst frightened a rabbitlike creature out of the grass. It hopped away in such obvious panic that Blade had to laugh.

He'd just stopped laughing when he heard a high-pitched droning from the direction of the river. He hurried down the bank to where he could hide in the grass and still look out at the river.

A hovercraft was cruising slowly along the main channel. It looked remarkably like a Home Dimension machine, with propellers mounted on top to drive it and a flexible skirt containing the air cushion under it. It looked battered, and there was some sort of lettering on the side. Like the yellow-green reeds, the lettering looked vaguely familiar to Blade. He strained his eyes, wishing he'd been willing to risk bringing on this trip a pair of binoculars. Some were all plastic, but all were obviously products of a high technology, and might have aroused suspicion in some Dimensions.

The hovercraft vanished behind a grove of trees before Blade could see more. When it reappeared, it was too far away for him to have any hope of making out the lettering.

Blade gritted his teeth. His first day in this Dimension was beginning to look like one of those days when everything goes wrong. It was particularly unpleasant to think about what might have happened to Cheeky.

At least he had one small consolation. The hovercraft showed that he was in a technologically advanced Dimension. It was a little less likely that Cheeky would be shot on sight as an evil spirit, or slaughtered, plucked, and popped into a cooking pot for some tribesman's dinner.

Another consolation for Blade was being able to

16

reach into his rucksack and pull out some food. He decided to eat it cold, rather than risk a fire. Where there was one hovercraft there might be others, and their crews might be armed and trigger-happy.

When he'd eaten, he curled up in his poncho, dry and almost warm. No hunting for a pile of dead leaves to put between his bare hide and the night winds this time!

If Cheeky had just been snuggled up under the poncho with him, Blade would have fallen asleep quite happily.

Chapter 3

Blade woke before dawn, feeling better than usual after his first night in a new Dimension. At least he felt better until he thought of Cheeky. Then he had to tell himself all over again that he wouldn't find Cheeky by worrying or blaming Lord Leighton.

Without leaving cover, he ate a chocolate bar and watched dawn break over the river. Several small boats passed slowly down the main channel, trailing fishing nets and lines. The fishermen wore broad-brimmed hats, and both men and women were bare to the waist.

From farther upriver a whistle sounded. Then a stern-wheel steamboat appeared, trailing a thick cloud of gray smoke. Her decks were crowded and she towed several heavily loaded barges. A boat the size of a large cabin cruiser followed in her wake, gliding along silently without noise or smoke. The fishermen waved as the two larger craft plowed past. The people aboard the steamer waved back.

Blade knew it was time to start moving. He wasn't going to find Cheeky or learn much about the Dimension by sitting here. The mix of technologies—steamboat, hovercraft, and rowboat—was odd but not unbelievable. He might be in some developing country or a land recovering from a nuclear war. Neither would be anything new.

He emptied one canteen, then headed for the stream to refill it. He was bending down when he heard the drone of propellers from high overhead. He looked up, and stopped with the empty canteen dangling from his hand to stare at what was approaching.

You could call it a flying train, if you had to find a handy name for it. The locomotive was a squarish metal box with a wedge-shaped nose that was mostly tinted glass. It looked rather like the cabin section of a helicopter with the rotors and tail cut off. Two large propellers whirled on outriggers near the nose. Two more were mounted aft, blowing over large rudders.

From between the rudders a long cable stretched astern, to the nose of a large sausage-shaped balloon. Three more balloons followed, tied nose to tail like railroad cars. A long gondola hung from each one. Blade saw shrouded piles of cargo, men moving among them, and guns at the bow and stern of each gondola.

The whole train made a weird sort of sense, if you assumed the "locomotive" was held up by some sort of antigravity. Certainly the propellers could never have done the job alone, nor could the balloons, which were brightly colored, in checkerboard patterns of yellow and green or blue and white. Each of them had what looked like a number on its bulging flank, and there was lettering on each gondola. It looked like the same tantalizingly familiar lettering Blade had seen on the hovercraft. It was also out of sight before Blade could get a good look.

On any previous trip, it would have been common sense for Blade to go where the balloon train was going. That way probably lay civilization—there, or along the river. On this trip, needing to think about Cheeky was changing all the rules.

Blade wouldn't even guess what the chances were that the feather-monkey was still alive. He'd made the transition into Home Dimension with Blade, but had he made it out the other side? And if he'd reached the same Dimension, had he landed anywhere close? Even if he'd landed only a few hundred yards away, he might have drowned in the marsh or the river.

Nonetheless, Blade was going to search at least the immediate area, if only because he would find it hard to live with himself otherwise. In fact, he was ready to spend most of his time in this Dimension hunting for Cheeky. The trip would be pretty much wasted if he *didn't* find Cheeky!

Even the immediate area along the riverbank was a pretty good-sized haystack, and he was looking for a needle with a mind of its own and the ability to move around. So the first thing to do was communicate with some friendly natives and get them to help him.

Not just any natives, though. Blade alone or Cheeky alone probably wouldn't appear suspicious. The two of them together could be. In a Dimension advanced enough to produce hovercraft and antigravity, the people would have many ways to discover the origin and identity of two such suspicious strangers. That meant danger to the Dimension X secret, and Blade's most important duty was always to protect that secret. He had to be ready to kill anybody or let himself be killed, rather than let anyone seriously suspect the existence of inter-Dimensional travel.

So he would have to find a community so isolated that even if they got suspicious, they might not be able to get word to the authorities or convince them if they did. It should also have so few people that he could kill them himself if necessary.

Blade devoutly hoped it wouldn't be necessary. He didn't *like* killing anybody, and certainly never peasants who probably wouldn't even know that they'd learned something dangerous. However, Blade was alive and sane after so many years as an agent and a traveler in far Dimensions because he could and would kill where necessary, as efficiently and ruthlessly as if he *did* enjoy it.

The first people he'd try were the fishermen on

the river. He wouldn't signal them from the bank, though. Such signals might attract other people's attention. Better to find a fishing village.

Blade looked back toward the wooded hill. From the top of one of those trees, he could see a good deal of countryside. Once he'd found the nearest fishing settlement, he could spy it out at night, then approach the people tomorrow morning. Being that careful would take a lot of time, when every hour counted, but not being careful—

Blade started to turn, then his instinct for danger suddenly flashed a warning: turn around *slowly*. He did so, keeping his hands well away from his sides and spreading out his fingers to show that he was unarmed.

Five men in green coveralls were standing among the trees. Four wore a variety of hats, and one a steel helmet. If they were soldiers, they must have armed themselves from a museum. One carried a crossbow, very much like Blade's except that the bow and winch were metal. Two carried what looked like turn-of-the-century army rifles with magazines and short thick bayonets. The man with the helmet carried a long-barreled pistol. The last man—Blade now saw it was a woman—carried something futuristic, made of what looked like black plastic.

One of the riflemen took Blade's stare as a hostile gesture. He raised his weapon and took aim. The helmeted man drew his pistol and knocked the barrel of the rifle up just in time. The bullet whistled over Blade's head. Before the man could fire again his leader was cursing him—and Blade stopped as if he'd grown roots.

He'd heard the language before. It was reaching his ears as English, thanks to the usual change in his brain as he passed into Dimension X. But he'd learned that if he concentrated and didn't try to translate, he could hear the original words clearly enough to recognize them.

The soldiers were speaking the language of Kaldak

21

and Doimar, the rival cities of a war-scarred Dimension groping its way back to civilization. He'd been there two trips ago. Before he left, he'd temporarily ended the rivalry by teaching Kaldak to use the ancient weapons of the fallen civilization, overcoming centuries of superstitious fear. Doimar's army was smashed, and at least a chance for recovery had been brought to the Dimension. It was one of his proudest accomplishments.

Now he was back in the same Dimension. A Dimension where he could easily be a legend, and which might have scientists who could learn the Dimension X secret from his return!

Chapter 4

Since doing anything right now would probably get him shot, Blade decided to do nothing. Getting himself killed here seemed a somewhat drastic way of protecting the Dimension X secret.

Blade slowly raised his hands and stood still. The crossbowman slung his weapon on his back and searched Blade. He took both knives and emptied the rucksack in search of more weapons. He didn't seem to find anything in the sack suspicious. Finally he put everything back and laid it at Blade's feet, with a gesture for Blade to put it back on.

Blade did so, feeling relieved. It didn't look like a case of "escape or die," at least for now. He could safely stay in these people's hands for a while. If they became friendly enough to talk to him—

But if they got that friendly and talk started, where would it end? How could he be sure the conversation wouldn't take a dangerous turn? He wouldn't have to actually reveal his identity, either. It would be enough to do something to make them suspect that he'd been in Kaldak before. Then they'd ask him where and when and why, and if there were any flaws in his answer . . .

He'd have to be more careful than usual to say as little as possible and get the other people to talk freely. He usually tried this anyway the first few days in a new Dimension, since it was the best and safest way of learning his way around. Now the stakes were higher. He'd be best off if he could get by without saying anything at all.

He could pretend to have lost his memory and not know who he was, where he was from, or where he was now. He'd done this before, and he doubted that anyone in this Dimension was as good at breaking cover stories or detecting acts as the Russian secret police, whom he had outwitted in the past. Once he'd learned what it was safe for him to be and to know, he could pretend to slowly recover his memory.

Of course if they shot amnesiacs like diseased animals in this Dimension he'd be jumping out of the frying pan into the fire! The Kaldakans hadn't done it the last time, though. He was willing to gamble they hadn't acquired the habit in however many years had passed here since then.

The five soldiers passed Blade's knives around and talked about them. This gave Blade a chance to make his face blank and relax his body until it would seem clumsy. His mind was anything but blank, however, and all his senses were even more awake than usual.

"All right," said the helmeted man. "Who are you, and why are you running around here in that clothing?"

Blade frowned. "Who am I?"

"I asked *you*." The man spat on the ground, but the woman frowned and pointed at herself.

"My name is Sparra." She pointed at the helmeted man. "He is Chyatho. He leads us."

"Leads?"

The rifleman raised his weapon, and this time Chyatho didn't stop him. "Who are you?" said Chyatho again, more harshly.

"I think—I am a man," said Blade slowly.

"You call that thinking?" said the rifleman, without lowering his weapon.

"Peace, Terbo," said the woman Sparra. "Perhaps it is the best thinking he can do." She stepped up to

24

Blade. "Bow your head." She repeated the words twice, then tried to show him what she meant. Seen from close up, she was attractive. Her figure was strong and full under her coveralls, and she had beautiful eyes and a wide, mobile mouth.

Blade, acting the part of a simpleton to the hilt, raised one hand and stroked Sparra's cheek. This almost got him more than he bargained for. Chyatho raised his pistol. The *click* as he cocked it made Sparra turn around.

"No, Chyatho!"

"Why not?"

"We do not know who he is yet."

"He is a man who touched you."

"You do not own me, even if I have given you a child."

"I should be able to keep other men away from you, at least."

"I can do that well enough myself, thank you."

"When you want to, yes."

"Of course. Sometimes I do not want to. You cannot make me want to, either. And none of this has anything to do with this man." She sighed. "Bow your head, stranger."

This time Blade obeyed. She searched his scalp, probing in his dark hair with long, sure fingers.

"Any injuries?" said Chyatho.

"There have been some, in the past," said Sparra. "This man has seen war, I think."

"Are they recent wounds?"

Slowly the woman shook her head. "Then stand aside, Sparra," snapped Chyatho. The pistol swung toward Blade. Terbo, the rifleman, Blade noted, was no longer aiming at him.

Sparra deliberately stepped in front of Blade. "You are a fool, Chyatho. Perhaps I would be better off if you did shoot me. There are many things beside head wounds which can make a man lose his memory. Fevers, great frights, the loss of someone he loves."

25

Some strong emotion passed over Terbo's face. "That is so," he said. "Also, we are on Bekror's land. He would not like to hear of our doing the Great Justice without letting him speak."

"Bekror will not speak to any purpose," said Chyatho. "And are you so sure we are on his land?"

"He will say we are," said the crossbowman. "I am sorry, Chyatho. But I think you are not wise, to want to kill this man simply because he touched Sparra. If the healers of Bekror's house can bring back his memory, we may learn something from him. Even if they cannot, Bekror will always be grateful for another strong slave."

"Are you all against me?" said Chyatho. His voice was almost a snarl.

"We are against you killing this man," said Sparra.

"What is—kill?" said Blade.

Chyatho threw up his hands in disgust, nearly dropping his pistol in the process. Then he holstered it. "Very well. We shall take him to Monitor Bekror. But we shall take him as if he had his wits about him, just in case." He pointed at Terbo and the crossbowman. "You two hold him while I bind his hands behind his back."

Blade submitted to the binding, but held his wrists stiff as the ropes went around them. Chyatho didn't notice. When he had finished, there was enough play in the bindings to let Blade free his hands in a couple of minutes.

He's risked breaking his cover by doing this, but he couldn't afford to be really helpless. He'd made a dangerous enemy in Chyatho, for no reason he could understand, and Sparra was in no position to be much of a friend.

He'd also learned hardly anything new about Kaldak. He didn't even know how many years had gone by since his first trip, which could be important. If everyone who'd known him personally was dead, his secret was a lot safer. About all he knew so far was that one squad of Kaldak's army had an odd assortment of weapons and no discipline worth talking about.

Monitor Bekror's establishment was a walled fortress the size of a small town. The area inside its walls covered several acres, with buildings, trees, pools, and gardens all mixed together.

Long ago, before the atomic war which destroyed the original civilization in this Dimension, there must have been a town here. Most of it was either destroyed in the war or crumbled into ruins afterward, when the population shrank. What must have been the town hall survived, though. It became Bekror's Great House, and the heart of his fortress. The walls had been reinforced with stone and stout gates, to make it easier to defend.

Blade's captors led him through one of the gates in the outer walls, past ragged sentries mostly armed with magazine rifles or crossbows. A more neatly dressed man with a pistol led the whole party through the maze inside the walls to the Great House. There Chyatho went inside, to learn if the Monitor would receive them today. The others waited outside, giving Blade a chance to study the weird contrasts all around him.

There was the door itself. It was twice as high as a man, of elaborately carved wood, and closed by a wrought-iron bar as thick as Blade's thigh. Above it in the wall was a niche, with two sentries on guard. They wore medieval-looking mail, but they sat by a water-cooled machine gun which might have come from the trenches of World War I. On top of the machine gun was something remarkably like a laser sight. Without moving his head, Blade could see five centuries of weapons and fortifications staring back at him.

By turning his head slightly, Blade could get even more confused. Of the five buildings in sight, two were log huts. One was a barracks, with soldiers coming in and out, and more sitting on the doorstep. Between the two huts was a large and thickly planted vegetable garden, with men and women working in it under the eyes of a couple of overseers. Both the men and the women wore nothing but loincloths. The people of Kaldak hadn't worried much about nudity the last time Blade was here; this didn't seem to have changed.

Of the three other buildings, one was stone like the walls, one was brand-new brick, and one was metal. The metal one was probably the oldest thing in sight. It was completely overgrown with vines and bushes and even small trees. The only clean spots were part of the roof and around the doorway. There the metal shone rustless and bright after what must have been centuries. Blade had the feeling that several Dimensions had all run together like puddles.

Eventually Chyatho came out, looking triumphant. Another guard came with him. "Monitor Bekror will see you now," the guard said.

Inside the hall, the first thing Blade saw was two clerks. Both wore monkish-looking robes and carried jewel-hilted daggers in their belts. One was using an adding machine, the other a crude tyepwriter. They sat in a cubicle hung with colorful tapestries. Just outside the cubicle four armed men sat on sandbags piled around a heavy laser, placed so that it could sweep the whole hall in a matter of seconds. The soldiers wore uniforms instead of chain mail, but they also carried sheathed swords. Blade had to listen to the language around him to remember that he was in Kaldak, or indeed in any place real.

Monitor Bekror met them seated at a long table at the far end of the hall. Several guards stood close by, but he obviously wasn't relying completely on them. He wore a shirt of plastic discs over leather, a sword, and a laser pistol.

How long has it been? Blade nearly shouted the

28

question out loud. Then he saw a large tapestry hanging on the wall over the Monitor's head. It showed a powerful dark-haired man flying above a ruined city on the strangest creature Blade had ever seen or imagined. It looked like one of the big metal waldos he'd learned how to control—the twelve-foot humanoid Fighting Machines. But it had a man's face on top of its metal body, and great feathered wings growing out of its back. Laser beams shot out of its eyes, and the man held a flaming sword.

This question he had to ask, risky as it might be. He pointed at the tapestry. "The—the High One?"

Sparra shook her head. "That is the Sky Master Blade."

Fortunately no one expected Blade to make a quick reply to that. He shook his head slowly. "The High One—I *know* him."

"Is that your name for the Sky Master?" said Sparra.

Chyatho made a disgusted noise. "Sparra, do not waste Minitor Bekror's time trying to get from this fool answers he will never give. Honored Monitor, we found this man on the bank of the Sclath." He told the story of Blade's capture. "I think Sparra hopes he may get back his wits. I do not. I think he has either lost them for good or is only pretending. If he is only pretending, we should learn what he really is."

Sparra had been fizzing like a glass of champagne while Chyatho spoke. Now she bubbled over. "Chyatho wants this man killed or tortured only because he touched me. Clearly Chyatho is so proud of the power of his loins in giving me a child that he wishes me to be his alone. I am sorry to have to shame him by saying this here, Honored Monitor. But I do not think you want to judge this man on Chyatho's word and nothing else."

The Monitor cleaned his glasses, pulled at his goatee, and scratched his heavy belly, then shook his head. "I do not. Chyatho, is what Sparra says true?

That you would bond with her by the New Law, not the Old?"

Chyatho sighed. "Yes. I have asked her a hundred times!"

"I have refused a hundred times, too," snapped Sparra. "If Chyatho were not a fool, he would have stopped—"

The Monitor raised a hand and thumped the table with the other fist. "Enough of your quarrel. My hall is not the place for it. By the power of justice given me under both the Old Law and the New Law, I give my judgment.

"I shall take this man into my care. If he can be taught to work, he shall work. Even if not, he shall not go naked or hungry. The Sky Master Blade taught us that when we have both the Oltec and the Newtec, it is wrong to let men starve who can be fed." Everyone in the hall bowed their heads at the mention of the sacred name "Blade."

"I shall also send to Kaldak for a truth-seeing machine. It is said that no man can hide his inner self from them."

"Would it not be wiser to send him to Kaldak?" said Sparra. "I would be glad to take him." Chyatho glared but said nothing.

"It is time that the rulers of Kaldak learned we of Sclathdon are their allies, not their slaves like captured Tribesmen," said Bekror sharply. "If they mean any of their promises to us, they will send the truth-seer here. If they do not, it is as well to learn now. If they do not want to learn about this man, the gardens can always use a strong man."

"But if he is lying, and has some dangerous plans—" began Chyatho.

Bekror raised his cup as if he wanted to throw it at Chyatho. "Use your brains instead of your balls for once, Chyatho! We are so far from Doimar that they could not have sent him without magic, let alone just Oltec! The Tribes have been peaceful, and does he look like any sort of Tribesman anyway?"

30

"No," said Chyatho, with a sigh.

"Very well. Then there is nothing he can do to harm us. That is my judgment, given by my power to take away your rank if you go on arguing."

Chyatho nodded stiffly. Blade rather wished the Monitor hadn't been so harsh. He'd probably guaranteed that Chyatho would take out his resentment on Blade the first time he thought he had a chance.

The Monitor signaled to his guards to take charge of Blade. They took his rucksack and knives, which made him uneasy for a moment, until he saw them given to Sparra—"spoils of the hunt," the Monitor said. As the guards led Blade out, he knew he'd learned something, although it wasn't exactly good news.

The Sky Master Blade was an almost divine figure in the history of this Dimension. If the people here learned that the man they held prisoner was the Sky Master himself, everyone would be curious about his return. Much *too* curious. They might not dare using the lie detector on him, but there would be a lot of questions asked. Scientists and engineers would be asking some of them. What would come of that? Nothing good for the Dimension X secret.

So—how safe was his identity? Apparently he was a long way from Kaldak, in an area brought under the city's rule since his first trip. Bekror seemed openly resentful of Kaldak's authority, in fact. It was unlikely that anyone here had ever seen the Sky Master Blade in the flesh, even if Blade's earlier trip to this Dimension was not so long ago that people who had seen him then were still alive today.

If he stayed out of Kaldak and away from lie detectors, he would probably be safe. He couldn't do much to find Cheeky while disguised as a feeble-minded farmhand, but at least he'd be doing the more important job adequately.

And who could say? He might find a way to do

both. Blade knew that as long as he was alive and alert, things could always change—sometimes even for the better. And at least he could hope to see trouble coming far enough in advance to run like hell, if that was the best he could do!

Chapter 5

As one of Bekror's farmhands, Blade had food, simple work, and plenty of chances to keep his eyes and ears open. It would have been hard to come up with a safer way of learning about this Dimension. Only the loss of Cheeky and the need to keep up the act of losing his memory spoiled the fun.

He finally decided that it must have been at least a generation since his last trip to Kaldak. He couldn't imagine so many changes taking place in less time. Of course the cold war with Doimar was still going on, and that sort of thing always pushed technology forward. It still took a certain amount of time to make the machines to make the machines to make the weapons! Twenty-five to thirty years at least, Blade guessed.

Since the Sky Master Blade came, there were two Laws in all the lands ruled from Kaldak, the Old Law and the New Law. Some people apparently preferred one, some the other. For example, under the Old Law women didn't have to be chaste or faithful. The custom arose in the days when most people were sterile. All the fertile ones had to get together sooner or later for there to be any children at all.

Under the New Law, a man who had fathered a child on a woman could ask her to remain faithful to him for life. Often she agreed. If she did the father was obliged to protect her and the child.

On the other hand, some mothers still preferred

their independence. Sparra was one of these. When a New Law man wanted fidelity from an Old Law woman, there was usually trouble. Blade only hoped he wouldn't get caught in the middle of any more of it.

There was also Oltec and Newtec. The Oltec—or old technology—was the same as last time: the knowledge and machines left over from the prewar civilization, such as the lasers and the power cells. In his last visit, Blade had helped the inhabitants of this Dimension relearn the use of these devices.

However, the superstitious fear of Oltec was gone. "The Sky Master Blade taught us wisdom" was the standard phrase. People could now repair a laser or recharge a power cell. They'd also rediscovered more Oltec which hadn't been used since the fall of the old civilization. The antigravity skytugs were the best example of that, although they were still rare.

They had also rediscovered minicomputers. Already Kaldak had Fighting Machines better, more compact, and more powerful than the old waldo robots. Before long these computers would be used by civilians; that clerk with his adding machine would be out of work within a generation at most.

There was also Newtec—what the Kaldakans had reinvented for themselves since the time of the Sky Master Blade. Most of the storehouses of Oltec were long since exhausted. There still weren't many places where new Oltec could be built or even repaired. It was much easier to build a hydrogen balloon and then tow it with a skytug, or build a steamboat and arm it with lasers, or build pistols, rifles, grenades, and mortars using plain old smokeless powder.

So the weird stew of technologies Blade saw around him actually showed a good deal of common sense and ingenuity on the part of the Kaldakans. He wondered how Doimar had done, with less prejudice against Oltec to begin with. However, since the two cities were still hostile, no one seemed to be willing to talk much about "the enemy."

34

It was really ironic. Blade had expected great things of the people of this Dimension once they got started on the road back toward civilization. They hadn't disappointed him either. But he couldn't possibly step forward and take any of the credit he deserved. That would threaten the Dimension X secret! Blade had to laugh.

When Blade went to bed, the moon was out. He could tell this from the spot of pale light on the floor of his cubicle. Like the other farmhands, Blade lived underground, in what he suspected was once an Oltec bomb shelter. Now it was divided into cubicles by brick and timber walls. Most of the farmhands slept two to a cubicle, but no one wanted to share a cubicle with a half-wit. Once they'd seen that Blade could take care of himself, they let him have a cubicle alone.

Over the centuries, the ground and the rubble of the building on the surface shifted. A shaft opened from the surface into Blade's cubicle. It would be a tight squeeze, but if he had to leave in a hurry he now had a line of retreat.

This let him sleep more easily at night. Not that he needed much help, after twelve hours' work and a heavy meal washed down with beer. The bed was crude but comfortable, too. Monitor Bekror was clearly the sort of master who believed that happy workers did their best. He was not one of the tyrannical masters who could drive their workers to the desperate step of running off to the Tribes.

The Tribes of mutants were much weaker now than the first time Blade came to Kaldak. Both of the great cities had expanded their lands. Where the cities ruled, the Tribesmen either died in the wars of conquest or fled beyond the reach of the cities.

Even then they still suffered losses. Sometimes they fought among themselves, larger Tribes with Newtec weapons devouring smaller ones. They exterminated the last pitiful bands of really serious mutants left over from the war. They even lost people raiding the outposts of the cities. Monitor Bekror's home had once been such an outpost of Kaldak, but it hadn't been attacked in five years. The lands of the Tribes were no more than two days' march away, but they seemed to have lost the will to fight.

Blade drank half the water in the jug on the floor by his bed and combed his hair with a comb of wire teeth set in a bone handle. The handle was carved into the form of a serpent. The craftsmen of Kaldak hadn't lost their habit of making even small household objects beautiful.

Then he used the rest of the water to wash the dust and dinner scraps out of his beard. He'd started growing one as soon as he saw it was allowed. Right now it was just long enough to make him look like a tramp. However, another week and even the people who'd seen him on the first trip would have trouble recognizing him. Certainly nobody here was going to recognize him from the portrait of the Sky Master on the tapestry in Bekror's hall!

If it hadn't been for the Dimension X secret, Blade would have been hoping that some of his friends from the first trip were still alive. His solitary life didn't give him friends that often. Chief Peython would probably be dead now, but what about his son, Bairam?

And Kareena—although she'd probably be a grandmother now, gray-haired and considerably older than Blade. He would still have liked to see her again. She had the combination of intelligence, courage, beauty, and the ability to stick up for herself he'd hope for if he ever looked for a wife again. After his experience with Zoé, he was afraid to do that again until after he retired—and what his chances of living that long were, God only knew. Certainly no life insurance company would have called Blade a terribly good risk!

He lay down on the bed and pulled the blankets over himself. He was just stretching out when he

36

noticed that the patch of moonlight on the floor was smaller than before. Had the moon gone behind a cloud? Then he noticed that the patch was changing both shape and size much too fast. Someone was crawling down the shaft from the surface.

Blade rolled over until he could get a good view of the ceiling. At the same time, he tried to look as if he were asleep or dozing. It would be out of character for him to be alert and ready for his visitor.

Now the moonlight was almost gone, and he could hear scrapings and scrabblings from overhead. A small pebble dropped out of the shaft and plopped into the water jug. Then a human figure followed it.

Blade wanted to laugh. Instead of a would-be assassin, perhaps Chyatho or someone sent by him, it was Sparra. She wore coveralls and her pistol, but had slung her boots around her neck. He recognized her at once, although she'd bound her dark hair under a scarf to keep off the dust of the shaft. She landed as lightly as a cat, looked around the room to make sure she was alone except for Blade, then undid the scarf. Her hair flowed down across her shoulders, framing her strong face. It shone glossy in the moonlight. Blade felt his breath quicken.

On her bare feet Sparra padded over to the bed and sat down cross-legged beside it. Then she lifted the blanket and ran her eyes down Blade's naked body. She seemed to like what she saw.

"Those scars—so many of them," she murmured. "If you were not a soldier or a hunter of dangerous game, I would like to know what you were. Will I ever know? Will *you* ever know, you poor lost man? Well, even now I know one thing. You were not born witless. Your blood is sound. I wonder about your loins, though."

Blade was also wondering about his loins; other parts of his body, too. He'd never before had to make love to a woman while pretending to be feebleminded. At least she didn't seem to expect him to be feeble-bodied as well. Perhaps if he—

"But you won't have had a woman for a long time, I suppose?" Sparra murmured. "No harm in that, but . . ." She ran nimble fingers up and down Blade's shaft, until it started to quiver encouragingly. Then without bothering to undress she bent over and enveloped the sensitive flesh with her lips.

Sparra's lips were as skilled as her fingers. That was Blade's first thought. It was also his last coherent thought for quite a while, as the pleasure Sparra was giving him swallowed him up. He couldn't have gone on acting if twenty scientists were standing around, ready to take notes on anything he let slip about the Dimension X secret.

Fortunately Sparra wasn't taking notes. Her partner's obvious arousal and pleasure increased her own. After Blade's first few gasps she drew back and pulled off her coveralls. Under it she wore a sort of body stocking, with buttons down the front. Then she went back to work.

A little bit later, she saw Blade's fingers beginning to writhe, as if he wanted to reach out and touch. "I think you remember *something*," she said, licking her lips. She unbuttoned the body stocking down to the waist. Blade reached out and cupped one of the full breasts. The dark nipple was already hard against his palm. He stroked it until Sparra threw her head back and gripped his wrist.

"Ah—n–n–no—too strong," and a few other things which made even less sense. Blade kept his hand in place, and after a while she let him go on. Her breast felt too good in his hand, and maybe his hand felt too good on her breast. *I wonder how long it's been since she was bedded?*

Then Sparra twisted clear, and pulled her garment down so that she was bare to the waist. Now Blade could reach one breast while she bent over him again and put her lips to work. The breast he couldn't reach, she kept pressing against him. When he finally groaned with release, she drank him down.

Then Sparra drew back and stripped off the rest

38

of her clothes. She stood in the patch of moonlight and turned slowly, knowing Blade's eyes were on her. He could tell she was no girl, and if he looked closely he could see the Stretch marks. Otherwise she was magnificent, with an all-over tan. Blade felt the beginnings of new arousal just looking at her.

She didn't wait for him, and he didn't expect her to. The lush triangle of dark hair between her thighs was already damp. She lay down on the narrow bed beside him, then rolled over on top of him. Her lips traced his eyebrows, then moved down over his cheeks and throat, while her hands chased each other over his ribs. . . .

She worked her way down until his new erection was cradled between her breasts. There she stayed, squeezing him firmly between the solid curves. She slid back and forth, and sometimes shifted to rub a nipple against Blade's rigid pulsing flesh.

At last Blade couldn't stand it anymore. He clutched Sparra by both shoulders and pulled her up onto him. He slid smoothly into her inner warmth, and she moaned. His hands clamped down on the solid buttocks, squeezing with more strength than tenderness as his own control faded.

It vanished entirely. So did Sparra's. They thrashed together in a tangle of arms and legs. Blade's groans mingled with Sparra's sobs of delight, as their sweat ran together and then flowed off them to soak the blankets.

After what seemed like an hour, the moment of release ended, and they lay still.

Sparra lay quiet on top of Blade so long that he was afraid she'd gone to sleep. He badly wanted to himself, but didn't want to be that rude to his partner. Besides, if someone came by and saw them together—well, Chyatho had been jealous enough over his simply patting Sparra's cheek!

At last Sparra's eyes flickered open. She raised her head and kissed Blade on the nose, then giggled. "Well, my friend. I thought your loins were sounder than your wits. I'm glad to know I'm still such a good judge of men. I wonder—were you a good judge of women, when you had your wits about you? Certainly you know your way around a bed."

Blade frowned, pretending to make a great mental effort. "I think—I *think* I had a—woman, wife? Anyway, when you touched me—I knew what I should do."

"You certainly did!" said Sparra unblushingly. "I hope you'll remember it, too, now that it's come back to you. I'm not going to use you up and throw you away after one night! No, by the Laws!" She wriggled up and bit his left ear hard enough to make Blade wince, then slid back down and rested her head on his stomach.

Blade let his fingers play with her tangled hair. He didn't mind Sparra being hungry for him—he'd seldom had a more satisfactory bed partner. But if the affair went on too long, Chyatho would notice. Before that happened, Blade knew he should be ready to escape from Monitor Bekror's estate.

Ideally he should find some place far enough from Kaldak to keep the Dimension X secret safe, but close enough to where he'd landed so that he could go on looking for Cheeky. He'd be damned if he was going to simply give up on the little fellow without a good fight!

It was easier to describe such a place than it would be to find it, though, but—wait a minute! What about the Tribes? They were close enough, certainly. They also had no science or technology worth mentioning, so they would be no danger to the Dimension X secret. If he told them that Cheeky was a magical animal, who would give them power against the Kaldakans. . . ?

Yes, but would the Tribes welcome strangers, or kill them on sight? Even if they let him in, how could he convince them that they should follow him anywhere, let alone in a war? And was Cheeky worth

40

setting the whole border country aflame and getting hundreds or thousands of people killed?

Reluctantly, Blade decided he was not. The feather-monkey was a friend as well as a valuable scientific experiment. He could not convince himself that Cheeky was worth a war. He would go to the Tribes if he had to escape Chyatho or the lie detector, but not try to enlist them in a search for Cheeky.

Back to square one. If he only hadn't pretended to have lost his memory—! But if he hadn't, he still couldn't have asked too many questions about Cheeky. If the Kaldakans weren't suspicious already, the feather-monkey could easily make them so.

Damn! Blade nearly said the word out loud. He wanted to get up and slam his fist against the wall in sheer rage and frustration. Then he saw that Sparra really was asleep, her arms around him and her legs drawn up. He ran his hand down the smooth skin of her back to the cleft between her buttocks. She wriggled like a kitten and smiled in her sleep. He wouldn't wake her up yet.

He went back to trying to find a way out of this trap. It didn't make any difference that he'd walked into the trap himself, or in fact that he really hadn't had much choice. The Dimension X secret had to be protected, and that was that.

He did know one thing. This was the last time he was going to risk having to sacrifice someone else to keep the secret. This time it had been Cheeky, which was bad enough. Next time it might be the first human companion to make the trip safely.

This decision might surprise Lord Leighton. He might even put it down as a weakness. It wouldn't surprise J, however, and he wouldn't attribute it to a weakness on Blade's part. Better than most, J knew that a good agent couldn't be a wild animal, that he had to have *some* scruples.

Gently Blade began to caress Sparra back to wakefulness. They would make love again, then he would somehow try to make her understand he

41

wanted to be alone. She would probably be ready for her own bed by then anyway.

One hand on her buttocks, the other creeping under her to stroke a breast. The nipple hardening, her eyes opening, a little gasp of pleasure, her solid flesh moving against his so that he felt his erection returning—

Someone screamed. It was faint and far off, but there could be no mistake about it. Then two more screams, and a shout.

"Tribesmen! Turn out, turn out! Tribes—!" and another scream ending in the gurgle of someone getting his throat cut. If you heard that sound once, you could never again mistake it for anything else— particularly when the first time, it was you doing the throat-cutting.

Blade sat up. Sparra rolled off the bed, nipples still erect and mouth still slack with desire. A sharp explosion sounded, then the crackle of a laser and several gunshots.

Now Blade heard a whole series of explosions and recognized them. Some were grenades, others mortar shells. Instead of his going to the Tribes, the Tribes had come to him. And they'd come much better armed than anyone around here seemed to expect.

Chapter 6

While Blade was figuring out what was going on, Sparra knelt naked on the floor, waiting for her arousal to fade. When it did, she pulled on her body stocking and belted the pistol over it. Then she sat down and started tugging on her boots.

Blade swung his feet over the edge of the bed and reached for his own clothes. Sparra shook her head. "No, my strong one. No. Bad men out there. They will hurt you. Hurt—*trouble*."

Being treated as a child just after he'd so thoroughly proved he was a man annoyed Blade. He let out an oath which made Sparra's eyes widen. Then he stood up and pulled on his pants.

"*Trouble* up there," she repeated, trying to push him back down on to the bed. She might as well have tried to push down a stone wall. Blade put an arm around her.

"It is like—when we were in bed. I hear the noise the bad men are making. I think I heard noises like this before. Then I knew what do do. Maybe I still do."

"You'll be no more than a lamb in the claws of a greathawk!" Sparra shouted. She seemed ready to weep with anger and frustration. "Stay down here and you'll be out of danger."

Blade knew that if a grenade or mortar shell came down the shaft, he would not only be out of danger, he would also be dead, and so would Sparra if she was still here arguing with him. By now he was fully dressed. The only weapon he had was his blunt-tipped pruning knife, but he'd armed himself from his enemies more often than he could remember.

Blade leaped high and swung himself up into the mouth of the shaft. Sparra muttered something about magnificent male animals too dumb to know danger when they should run away from it, but followed him.

Blade didn't know how to climb the shaft quickly and still look confused, so he didn't try. He took the shaft as fast as he could. On the surface he and Sparra had a chance, even if the Tribesmen overran the whole estate. They would not be rats in a trap.

By the time Blade reached the surface, a pitched battle was raging all over the estate. Explosions, laser blasts, individual gunshots and the rattle of machine guns, shouted orders and screamed rage and agony—everything blended into one continuous deafening uproar.

Sparra poaked her head out of the shaft, heard the din, and swallowed hard. Sweat broke out on her forehad. She looked on the edge of panic. Blade remembered tales of what the Tribesmen did to City women. He also remembered what one band of Tribesmen had nearly done to Kareena, before he killed them.

He bent down, gripped her by the hair, and pulled her face up to his. "No *fear*," he said sharply. "I know what to do now. Give me your—" He pointed at her pistol, pretending not to know the word for it. She shook her head.

"You—"

"Get down!" Blade shouted, pushing her back into the shaft and flinging himself over the mouth. The whistle of the incoming mortar shell rose to a deafening screech. A moment later the explosion crashed against Blade's ears. Fortunately it seemed to come from the other side of the wall to his left.

Then the wall sagged, split and cracked into its

original stones, and collapsed. The roar drowned out the battle, and the dust was so thick Blade could hardly see ten feet. He lay across the mouth of the shaft until the wall subsided into a pile of rubble, in spite of Sparra's curses from below.

As the dust cloud thinned, Blade saw that at least one of the estate's defenders had been unlucky. The man lay across one block of stone with another on his legs. From the way he was lying, Blade knew his back was broken and his legs crushed. His magazine rifle lay intact beside him, though. so did an ammunition pouch. Blade scooped them up, while the man whimpered and begged someone to kill him. Sparra now had enough control of herself to do as he asked.

Her pistol shot seemed to waken the battle around them again. Something exploded among the tumbled stones of the wall. This time Sparra didn't need urging to hit the dirt. Blade stayed down until he'd inspected the rifle. As he'd thought, it was very much like an early twentieth-century army rifle—bolt-action, with a rectangular magazine holding seven rounds. He'd won marksmanship contests with an Enfield not too different from this; he knew he could make himself unpleasant to the Tribesmen with it.

Then Sparra's pistol went off almost in his ear. He looked up and saw dark figures running toward them across the rubble. Or at least they were trying to run. The bad footing reduced them to an undignified stumble. It also slowed them considerably. Sparra fired again, and shouted to Blade, "Tribesmen, you idiot! Or were you one of them?"

Blade started shooting. He dropped two men before the others started to duck, and a third as he spent a little too long looking for cover. Then bullets whistled around Blade as the others opened fire. The shooting seemed fairly random, but Blade was afraid of ricochets off the stones lying all around.

He put his mouth close to Sparra's ear. "We'll have to stay down for a bit. If they charge, you go back down the shaft. I can hold them off better with the rifle."

She looked at him, dark eyes enormous in a face pale with caked dust. She seemed bewildered at Blade's transformation from half-wit into soldier. Well, there'd be time enough to sort things out if they both lived through the night! At least he was doing his fighting in front of a witness who *might* be persuaded to keep her mouth shut.

Blade refilled the magazine from the loose rounds, found another filled magazine in the pouch, and put that ready to hand. He now had fourteen rounds ready to stand off any rush by what looked like less than ten men. With Sparra's pistol as well, that should be enough, even in the darkness. Blade would still have given a lot for a submachine gun or one of the laser rifles.

The rifle fire from the Tribesmen began to die away. Blade heard scrabbling noises and hoped they were retreating. The battle noise continued, but now from farther away. It sounded as if the Tribesmen had attacked simultaneously all around the estate, hoping to overwhelm the defenders by surprise and sheer weight of numbers. Now that the defense was rallying, they were moving their new attack to where the first rush had found weak spots. That was better tactics than Blade had ever heard of the Tribesmen using. Either they'd found a war chief who knew modern warfare, or they were getting leadership as well as weaponry from Doimar. Neither was a very pleasant idea.

Blade again suggested that Sparra should go back down the shaft. "They'll need word of how things are here," he pointed out.

"Yes, but if the Tribesmen attack again and kill you, things will change. So my information will be useless back at the Great House. My gun will not be useless here."

Blade gave up. Sparra was a soldier with a sense of duty just as strong as his, not a woman to be protected. At least she'd adjusted to the idea that he could be treated as a rational adult. He'd have to be careful, though, not to make it appear that his memory was coming back *too* fast.

Then a steamboat whistle sounded from the river, and a rocket shot up against the sky, trailing green fire. A moment later the darkness gave way to dazzling white light, as a cluster of flares burst high over the estate.

Blade counted at least a dozen Tribesmen in sight. Some flinched at the glare, then froze in position. Others, less well trained, jumped up. Among them were two carrying a thick black tube on a tripod. To Blade, it looked like a heavy laser. Snap-shooting, he picked off one of the men. The other stayed up a little too long, trying to keep the laser from smashing on the rocks. Blade's second shot and Sparra's pistol bullet hit him almost together. He went down, and the laser fell on top of him.

"Cover me," whispered Blade, handing the rifle to Sparra. Then he dashed across the rubble toward the laser. Surprise kept the Tribesmen from shooting until he was picking it up. The first shots were wild, and Sparra picked off two men who rose to aim better. Then the flares died, and before the Tribesmen's eyes could readjust to the darkness Blade was back under cover with his prize.

"That's Doimari Oltec," said Sparra grimly. She examined it. "And it's fully charged, too. I think—" She broke off to shoot at a Tribesman who'd jumped up and was running off to the left. He screamed and went down.

"I hope you got him," said Blade. "I think he was a messenger, sent to warn reinforcements that we've got the laser. If you got him, they may be walking right into our sights in a bit."

"And if a message gets through?"

"Then we'll probably have mortars or grenades coming over soon. You're sure you don't want to get away while you still can?"

She bit him gently on the ear. "No—and do you remember your name now, my friend? If I am going to die with you, I'd like to know it."

"Call me Voros. That sounds more right than anything else."

"All right, Voros. I don't care what the Laws or the Monitor might say, I would always think I was a coward if I left you now." Blade squeezed her hand, and they settled down to wait, no longer a man and a woman but just two infantrymen waiting for the enemy.

They didn't have to wait long. A whistle blew in the darkness, then a more solid part of that darkness began to move toward them. As it came closer, it broke up into individual Tribesmen, their faces and ragged clothing darkened but each holding a shiny new rifle. Some of the rifles even had bayonets. Moving out ahead of them was a single figure with a whistle on a cord around his neck and a short-barreled laser in his hand. Blade held his breath. If anyone warned that officer even now—

No one passed the word, and the Tribesmen paid for it. As the Tribesmen who'd taken cover rose to join their comrades, Blade raised the laser and opened fire. His first blast hit the officer and the whole squad behind him. One of them must have been carrying demolition charges. He exploded as the laser hit him, and grisly pieces of his body rained down. The squad behind him froze, and Blade cut them down before they could move. Then both he and Sparra were firing into the confused mass of men coming on behind the two point squads.

Perhaps the Tribesmen were new warriors who'd never before faced point-blank laser fire. Or perhaps the surprise and the loss of their officer confused them. In any case, they turned and ran after only a minute of Blade's laser work. They fired a few wild shots, but after another demolition man blew up they stopped doing even that. Five minutes after the attack began, it was over. There wasn't a living

48

Tribesman in sight, except a few moaning wounded, writhing among the far more numerous corpses. The stench of burned flesh and ozone was strong enough to turn even Blade's cast-iron stomach.

In the silence Blade heard the steamboat whistle again, then the hiss and crackle of heavy lasers. "That's probably the City Regiment from Kaldak," said Sparra. "Late as usual, and of course they won't come in here. They'll go off chasing the Tribesmen, and try to get the glory without doing any real fighting."

"There's something to be said for that, It's always risky, new troops moving into a battle area at night. Easy to make mistakes and shoot your friends."

Sparra frowned. "That is true. It is also more than I really expected you to know about war. What *were* you?"

Blade realized that he'd said a little too much, but luck saved him the need of replying. A hail came from out of the darkness.

"Hoaaaa! Is anyone there?" It was Chyatho's voice.

"It's Sparra," she called back. "The Tribesmen tried to come through here. But the man who'd lost his memory—Voros, he calls himself—he'd captured one of their lasers. He *butchered* them, Chyatho."

Blade heard mutterings, then from someone else, "By the Laws, she's right. You can't see the ground for the dead, some places."

Chyatho came forward, his pistol drawn, leading a squad. Blade recognized Terbo the rifleman and the crossbowman from the squad by the river. Then Chyatho noticed Blade's laser and Sparra's lack of clothing. His face hardened.

"What have you two been doing, besides killing Tribesmen?"

"Nothing," said Sparra. Blade stood silently. Chyatho was only too obviously carrying a big chip on his shoulder. Blade's suddenly revealing his newly regained wits could provoke him even more. It would be better if Sparra handled the matter.

"Nonsense!" said Chyatho.

"Nonsense?" repeated Sparra. "What else do you think we've had time to do?" She waved a hand at the bodies of the Tribesmen.

"She's right, Chyatho," said Terbo. "Now calm yourself and let's start—"

"No, before that!" shouted Chyatho. Blade quietly shifted his footing, to be ready if the man attacked. His voice was ugly. "You were gone long enough to do anything you damn well pleased, the way you always do!"

"I swear by the Law that I have taken or given away nothing which was yours," said Sparra coldly. Blade rather wished he could slip away in the darkness, because this quarrel could do him no good. But if he vanished, Chyatho would probably take his anger out on Sparra.

Chyatho wasn't too angry to notice Blade's stance. "He's listening and understanding what we say!" he screamed. "He was lying, and so are you, bitch!"

Terbo grabbed Chyatho's shoulder. "Come on, Chyatho! It's been a long night, and you're half out of your mind—"

Chyatho let out an animal's screech, twisted out of Terbo's grasp, and hurled himself at Sparra. Before Terbo could draw his pistol, Chyatho was too close to the woman for him to fire without danger of hitting her.

With only his bare hands, Blade wasn't similarly handicapped. He caught Chyatho in a judo hold and the man shot up over Blade's shoulder with a yell of surprise and fear. Unfortunately, he twisted half out of Blade's grip in mid-flight. Blade had intended to drop him on a patch of soft earth to the left of the shaft mouth. Instead Chyatho landed head-down on a solid lump of rock. Everyone heard the sickening double crunch as his neck snapped and his skull caved in.

Terbo knelt by Chyatho for a moment, to make sure he was dead, while Sparra covered the other men with the laser. From her expression, it was

50

obvious that any man who batted an eye was likely to get a laser beam through his guts.

Finally Terbo rose and looked hard at Blade. "You have got your wits back, haven't you?"

There didn't seem to be any point in lying. "Enough to remember I was a fighting man, and most of what I knew when I was."

"Then I'm afraid I'll have to ask you to hand over your weapons."

"Why should I trust you?" said Blade.

"No reason, except you can trust me more than some of the other men. Chyatho had a good many friends. If I take your weapons and put you under my protection, none of them will dare touch you until Monitor Bekror himself has given his judgment. Otherwise you may find yourself fair game, with a lot of hunters around. How many eyes and ears do you have?"

"Do what he says, Voros," said Sparra. "He's rough-spoken but I've never known him to break an oath, even to an enemy." she added in a tight whisper that only Blade heard, "I've caused Chyatho's death to-night. I don't want to see you die, too."

"All right," said Blade. He reversed the rifle and handed it butt first to Terbo. Something flying droned overhead, and green laser light flared off to the left, followed by machine-gun fire. Then darkness and silence returned.

Chapter 7

Blade spent the rest of the night in an informal sort of protective custody. Sparra took command of Terbo's squad and led it off into the darkness while Terbo himself mounted guard over both Blade and the body-strewn rubble.

That worried Blade. If he was in danger of death from Chyatho's friends, what about Sparra? He probably couldn't do anything to help her tonight, but it was always better to know for sure things like this.

"You and she did get together, didn't you?" was Terbo's reply. "And don't lie."

"We did," said Blade.

"I thought so, That phrase of Sparra's—'nothing which is yours'—I've heard it before. So has Chyatho. This must have been one too many times."

"Whose side are you on?"

"The side of not getting any more good fighters or live loins killed tonight," said Terbo. "That's why I'm protecting you. It's also why I will hunt down any man who touches Sparra for this night's work if the Monitor doesn't do it first."

"Are you—claiming Sparra—now that Chyatho is dead?" As long as he was pretending to recover his wits, he could ask what would otherwise have been stupid questions.

"I am not," said Terbo. "You see, I am dead-loined. I can be a Protector to the children other men father, but never put one into a woman myself. Sparra

52

has borne Chyatho a son, and is young enough to bear more to another man with live loins. It would go hard with both of us if I claimed her. Oh, I have bedded her at times when both of us were in need. But I would not claim her. I advise you not to, either, at least until you have all your wits back. She will say ten words to your one, otherwise."

Blade laughed. "So I suspected."

After that they talked freely. Terbo had been a soldier for more than twenty of his forty years. In fact, he'd fled as a boy from a village overrun by the Doimari advancing to the great battle where the Sky Master Blade defeated them. With both parents dead he was adopted by a Kaldakan family, then went into the army as soon as he was old enough for them to take him. Since then, he'd fought in most of Kaldak's major battles and a good many of the minor ones, in several different units of Kaldak's army.

"Not the City Regiment, though. Never those high-nosed types. They don't take village boys," he added. He sounded more resigned than bitter.

"The City Regiment?" Blade recalled hearing Sparra mention it, after they heard the steamboat whistle and saw the rocket.

"We call them the Sitting Regiment, out here," said Terbo.

Most of Kaldak's fighters were local-defense troops, under local control and armed with whatever came to hand. In fact, some of the cities and districts which joined Kaldak did so on the condition that they maintain their own armed forces. Monitor Bekror's troops were one of those almost feudal private armies.

Then there were the five battalions of the City Regiment, crack troops armed with the best Oltec *and* Newtec. They rode in hovercraft, flew in balloons, dropped by parachute, and controlled robotic Fighting Machines. They were the strategic reserve, held back most of the time and thrown in only when a situation got beyond what the local troops could handle.

Then they fought well. Even Terbo would admit as much. They were brave and could use their weapons with devastating skill. What Terbo and men like him resented was the feeling that they were used as bait. "We suck 'em in, anyone the High Commander wants flattened. We take all the pounding. Then the Sitters come charging out, do all the damage, and get all the glory."

The quarrel between elite troops and the ordinary infantryman went back as far as war itself, Blade knew. He remembered how the war effort of Doimar was nearly wrecked from the start by the quarrel between the regular soldiers and the scientists who controlled the Fighting Machines. He wondered what happened in Doimar after the battle, when the Seekers withdrew the Fighting Machines and left the infantrymen to fight or die. It couldn't have done any fatal damage, or Doimar wouldn't still be a menace.

It didn't help that between battles the City Regiment was close to civilization and all its comforts. "When they're not training, they'll be sitting on a cushion with a girl on their laps and good liquor in their cups. When we're not training, we're building bridges and roads, clearing rubble, harvesting crops, things like that."

Blade nodded sympathetically. The conversation died away as they waited for dawn.

Dawn brought a squad of the City Regiment, men and women in blue uniforms, all armed with laser rifles and led by a tall woman with hard yellow eyes which didn't miss much. They took over Blade's position and chased him and Terbo out almost as if they'd been Tribesmen. Blade was happy to go. The smell of death was getting too thick, and he was hungry.

Blade learned about the battle from listening to

the talk in the barracks over breakfast. The Tribesmen had surprised the estate because nobody was expecting them. An even bigger surprise was their Doimari weaponry, both Newtec and Oltec.

However, the City Regiment must have somehow known about the attack in advance. Their Fourth Battalion had been ready on riverboats an hour's steaming upstream. As soon as they got word of the attack, they came in. Thanks to the determined resistance by the people on the estate, the Tribesmen were still concentrated around it when the Fourth arrived. Less than half the Tribesmen got away, and those who had were being chased.

It was "a famous victory." Or at least it would be, when the damage was repaired, the dead were buried and forgotten, and everybody stopped worrying about the Doimari assistance to the Tribesmen. Everyone wondered if the rival city was starting the war again in earnest.

Everyone also seemed to know that Blade had his memory back, and that he'd done heroic work against the Tribesmen. Many also seemed to know about Chyatho's death. Blade got a mixture of congratulations which he accepted and black looks he did his best to ignore.

After breakfast, a messenger summoned him to the Monitor's hall. Bekror was red-eyed with fatigue and grief. He'd been up all night, in the thick of the fighting for most of it. One of his sons was dead, and one of his daughters had miscarried as a result of the attack.

However, his voice was brisk and steady as he spoke to Blade. "You did the work of seven men last night, Voros," he began. "You will be rewarded for it, whatever you decide."

"I—decide?" said Blade. He wasn't entirely pretending to be confused.

"Yes. You got your memory back last night, didn't you?"

"Some of it, sir."

"Do you remember where you came from?"

"No. I don't think it was one of the big cities, but that's all I can even guess."

"So I heard. If you had come from around here and had kin who could avenge you, you could stay and be well protected. The Laws know I would gladly keep you around. Or you could return home. But you have no home, and it's just not safe for you to stay here."

"It's Chyatho's death, isn't it?"

"Terbo has been talking, hasn't he?"

"Yes."

The Monitor shrugged. "I don't blame him for talking or you for listening. The only way you could have shut him up was by strangling him, and he probably told you the truth anyway. Beer?" He held up a pitcher.

Blade shook his head. Although he'd eaten a large breakfast, he still felt light-headed with fatigue.

The Monitor poured himself a cup and drank, then went on. "I keep to the Old Law, myself. A man and a woman can get together as they wish, as long as they have her mate's or father's consent. I try to make everyone who serves me keep to the Old Law, too.

"But years pass and things change. Now there are men who follow the New Law, which says a woman *must* be faithful to the man who gives her a child. Or says he gave her children," he added, swallowing more beer. "The New Law is a gift to any liar who wants to make his woman a slave. I do not understand why any man could wish children from a woman who would bow like that, but then I grew up under the Old Law. I was the father of three children by three different women before the Sky Master Blade came." Another swallow.

"Chyatho led those men of my lands who wanted the New Law followed here. He had a good many friends, or at least people ready to avenge him. I cannot protect you forever from all of them, particu-

56

larly not if you're going to be in any more fighting. In battle, it's easy to make murder look like an accident or the enemy's work."

Bekror drained the cup and refilled it. "However, there's a way for you to leave here with honor and find safety. The Commander of the Fourth Battalion of the City Regiment has asked if you would like to volunteer for the Regiment. Most of the time, I'd secede from Kaldak before I let a man as good as you go to the Sitters. That's how they keep up their strength—sucking all the best blood away from where it's really needed. But you're a special case. What do you say, Voros?"

Seeing Blade hesitate, the Monitor added, "I don't know what you think of the Sitters, but they do know how to fight. The Fourth particularly. You may remember that they're called Kareena's Own."

Blade managed to suppress a violent start into a small one. "Kareena?"

"Peython's daughter, who was consort to the Sky Master Blade. You know the name?"

"It seems—familiar."

"You probably had a girl named after the original one. The Laws know there were enough of them, for a couple of years after she was killed."

"Killed?"

"You don't remember the story? Well, Kareena was leading the Fourth when they got into a Doimari ambush. She took the rear guard and held off the Doimari long enough for most of her people to get away. She was hurt and told the rear guard to leave her, but one of them stayed with her. She played dead, but hid a grenade under her body. When the Doimari came to get her, she pulled the pin and blew up about a dozen of them along with herself."

"That sounds like—"

The Monitor interrupted before Blade could say anything too revealing. "I don't wonder if it sounds familiar. If your girl was named after Kareena, she must have sucked in the story with her mother's

57

milk." He swallowed more beer. "Why don't you take a walk and think it over? Don't go too far, though. I don't think Chyatho's friends would try anything with the Fourth all over the place, but why take chances?"

Why indeed? thought Blade, as he walked along the riverbank an hour later. Overhead the sky was gray, matching Blade's mood.

Which *was* taking unnecessary chances, going or staying? If he stayed, he would have an honorable place in Bekror's service. He might even be able to find some subtle way of hunting for Cheeky.

However, Cheeky was probably dead or hopelessly lost. The search could be a waste of time. Or the Tribesmen might attack again and he could never make it at all. Meanwhile, he would have to guard his back from Chyatho's friends day and night.

If he went to join the Fourth Battalion, he would have another kind of honorable place, in the crack troops of Kaldak. He should be safe from Chyatho's friends. He would not be able to search for Cheeky, but he would certainly learn a lot more about what was going on in this Dimension.

He would have to go to Kaldak, then, even though he might wind up facing someone who'd known the Sky Master Blade. And he would be serving in "Kareena's Own," where he'd face reminders of her every time he turned around. He wondered if she'd had his child safely. That would be a little too much to ask outright here, but in the ranks of the Fourth Battalion he might learn without having to ask.

It helped him feel better to know that she'd died like a soldier, and been spared another ordeal as a Doimari prisoner. She could never have survived it, not after her first time in their hands.

A platoon of soldiers from the Fourth marched past. Blade noticed that their blue uniforms were clean but well worn. These weren't parade-ground soldiers. Their weapons were also shining and bright, and some of the men wore beards. All of them marched as if they not only knew they were the best but wanted the whole world to know it.

There could be worse ways to spend a trip to Dimension X than serving in the ranks of a good fighting outfit. If he could keep his beard, he might not even have to worry about being recognized in Kaldak.

In his mind Blade said good-bye to Cheeky, and after a moment another good-bye to Kareena. Then he started up the bank, toward Bekror's gate.

Chapter 8

Sparra's legs clamped hard around Blade, and she let out a long groan of delighted release. A moment later Blade echoed her.

They lay locked together until the sweat dried off. Blade raised himself on one elbow and looked along Sparra's solid, well-curved brown body. Then he traced with one finger the path his eyes had followed.

"I'm going to miss you," he said. This was quite true. It was equally true that he'd got used to a life which was just one good-bye after another.

"And I you," said Sparra, gripping his hand and pulling it against one breast. "Were things otherwise, I would gladly take you for my man. But it would not be seemly, even though Chyatho was killed more by his own rage than by your hands. Also, it would make more danger for you."

It would probably be damned close to signing his death warrant, Blade knew. Aloud he said, "It might make Chyatho's friends turn against you as well. Without me around, they may not risk angering Monitor Bekror."

"I will save the money you have given me," she said. "It will be enough to let me start in another part of the land in case Chyatho's friends cause trouble for me and I must leave Sclathdon."

The Monitor had given Blade a year's pay that morning. Blade promptly gave three-quarters of it to Sparra. He was also leaving his gear with her. She didn't want it, but he wouldn't need it in the Fourth Battalion. Also, the farther it stayed from Kaldak and its curious scientists the better.

"Good luck," he said.

"I wish you the same. You are more likely to need it."

Blade grinned. "In the Sitting Regiment?"

"There will be more fighting in the next few years than there has been since the Great Doimari War, I think."

"Others do not think so," said Blade cautiously, to draw her out on the military situation.

"Others do not see even what jumps up and hits them in the face," said Sparra. She sat up, arms crossed over her breasts, eyes wide with indignation. "They say that Feragga of Doimar is old and wants peace. Perhaps they are right. But can they be sure that what Feragga wants is what Doimar will do? She may be so old that they ignore her. A whole generation of Doimari has grown up since the war. They have shame to avenge, and we do not have the Sky Master Blade this time."

"You seem to have much of what he taught you," said Blade. So that shrewd amazon Feragga had survived! He'd last seen her in the arms of a Fighting Machine, being carried away over the hills while her War Leader Nungor covered her retreat at the cost of his own life. She must be well into her seventies now. He could easily believe that she wanted peace.

Unfortunately, he could also believe that she no longer had enough power in Doimar to bring it about. The arming of the Tribesmen was certainly no peaceful gesture!

"Yes. But will it be enough?" said Sparra grimly.

Since he had no answer to that, Blade kissed her, and they wound up making love again. Then they slept until late afternoon, when a servant came to summon Blade to the waterfront. As the sun set, he boarded the steamboat as Recruit Private Voros of the Fourth Battalion, City Regiment of Kaldak.

61

*   *   *

To make it easier to feed and house them, each Battalion of the City Regiment was based in a different city. Since each Battalion had its own balloons, hovercraft, and Fighting Machines, each one could fight a fair-sized battle all by itself. If more than one Battalion was needed, it could be called by radio and quickly moved by balloon and riverboat. Apparently no one in this Dimension had invented the railroad.

The Fourth Battalion was quartered in Gilmarg, the city where Blade found the vast hoard of power cells which helped Kaldak start its climb back to civilization. It was a strange and not a completely pleasant sensation, wandering the streets where he'd met the first of the Doimari Fighting Machines and dueled to the death with the arrogant warrior Hota.

It was definitely not pleasant to stand by the site of the building where the power cells had been hidden. Far below it was the underground shelter where he and Kareena first made love. In the busy street on either side of him the Doimari ambushed and captured them, raping and torturing Kareena. Then the Doimari set off the booby traps Blade left behind, and the building collapsed on its treasure house of Oltec.

The Kaldakans dug it all out many years ago, and built on the site. You could even take a guided tour of the underground shelter if you wanted to. Blade didn't, and after one visit he stayed away from the street altogether. He wasn't sure if it was the ghosts there or the feeling that he was a ghost himself, but either way he didn't like it.

He didn't have that much time for playing tourist, in any case. The training was rigorous, although Blade quickly passed out of the Recruit's course and was sent on to the Advanced Infantry School. Everyone knew that he'd been a soldier before he lost his memory, so no one saw anything particularly odd in this.

He still had to keep his wits about him. Working

62

with the new Fighting Machines, for example, wasn't quite like working with Home Dimension tanks. The Fighting Machines were miniature hovercraft, each armed with a grenade launcher and a powerful laser. Some also had machine guns. On the march, a man rode in each one and steered it. In combat, the Fighting Machines were controlled by radio, or could even be programmed to operate on their own.

Otherwise, Blade led the usual life of a new recruit in any well-run military outfit. He had plenty of time to listen to the talk around him. Bit by bit, he filled in the gaps in his knowledge of what had happened in Kaldak and which of the people he'd known had survived.

He knew Kareena was dead in battle. Her father, Peython, was also dead, apparently of pure old age. Sidas had married Kareena, then remarried after her death. He was still alive; in fact he was the High Commander of the armed forces of Kaldak. Blade was glad to hear that. Sidas had a rare combination of ingenuity, courage, and common sense.

Kareena's brother, Bairam, had married the merchant Saorm's daughter, Geyrna, and produced a fine family. Then after his father's death he got into some sort of trouble—Blade couldn't learn the details. In any case, he was now in polite exile in a remote part of Kaldak's empire. Geyrna divorced him and was now a member of the Council of Nine, the highest political body in Kaldak.

Blade was glad to discover that so many of his friends had survived and done well. He was sorry about Bairam, but "trouble" sounded like just the sort of thing he might have expected. Bairam probably never did learn to keep his mouth shut!

Still, it would be wiser to stay out of Kaldak as much as he could. If he couldn't do that, he could at least avoid making himself conspicuous. He realized he'd been very lucky with his heroism at the estate. It only got him a chance at anonymity in the City Regiment, instead of a call to Kaldak for public honor.

The lie detectors and computers in Kaldak sounded much too good for Blade's comfort. If they once got the idea that travel into other Dimensions was possible . . .

However, nothing could make Blade stop looking for opportunities. A good secret agent needs among his other qualities the persistence of an ant or a door-to-door salesman, and Blade had been one of the best. He kept his eyes and ears open. He wasn't optimistic, particularly about doing anything to find Cheeky, but he declined to curl up into a little ball.

The thing he hoped most to learn was the fate of his child by Kareena. "Kareena's daughter" was mentioned occasionally, but quietly and cautiously, as if she'd committed some disgraceful crime. It was impossible to tell who her father was, the Sky Master Blade or Commander Sidas.

Before Blade could learn more, the Fourth Battalion was off to war again.

Chapter 9

The dim light in the tail of the antigravity sky-tug suddenly blinked twice. The sergeant in the bow of the balloon gondola unhooked the towing cable and let it drop away into the night. The whine of the tug's propellers died away, and the three balloon-loads of Fourth Battalion paratroopers were alone in the silent darkness.

"Count off," came the word, in whispers. They were a good mile up and several miles from the nearest Tribesmen, so it really made no sense to whisper. A hundred-and-twenty Fourth Battalion infantrymen rode in the three balloon gondolas. Now that the tug had cast off, they were drifting before the wind.

If the wind cooperated, the balloons would drift toward an important Tribesman village. According to aerial reconnaissance, the village held much of the ammunition and weapons sent by the Doimari for the Tribesmen in the area. It might even hold a few Doimari advisers.

Parachuting from balloons drifting silently in the night sky, the Kaldakans hoped to surprise the village. The ammunition and weapons would be destroyed, the advisers captured.

Then the company would dig in and wait for a Kaldakan offensive against the Tribesmen between the village and the border. Faced with Fighting Machines and artillery, the Tribesmen would have to retreat. Their main line of retreat lay through a pass controlled by the village. They would be retreating right into the company's arms.

At least that was the plan, as Blade understood it from the briefing. He also understood how many things could go wrong with it, and how fatal some of them could be to the isolated company. Since he was supposed to be a new recruit, about to jump into his first battle with the Fourth Battalion, he kept his mouth shut. It wouldn't do for him to be caught thinking like a combat veteran and an officer.

At least he would be down on the ground, not up here with the balloon crews. Infantry combat was nasty, vicious, and dangerous, but you still had solid ground under your feet and usually some place to hide. The balloon crews would fight their battle high in the sky, hanging helplessly from a couple of million cubic feet of highly explosive hydrogen. Even if they took to their parachutes, they weren't necessarily out of the woods. They could land in wilderness and die of starvation, or land among Tribesmen and be tortured to death.

Even in the civilized lands, few lights showed on the ground at night. Here in the Tribal lands it was like looking down into a bottomless pit. Far away Blade saw what might have been a campfire, or maybe just the reflection of the half-moon on a pond.

Finally the order came to hook up. Blade clipped the static line of his parachute to the cable which ran around the edge of the gondola. Then he began to breathe slowly and steadily, to relax himself. He'd made more than forty parachute jumps, some in combat, but he still got a few butterflies in his stomach before each one. You were just as dead if your chute failed on the hundredth jump as on the first.

"Five—four—three—two"—by alternate numbers— "*jump!*" came the sergeant's growl.

Dark shapes began hurling themselves over the edge and plummeting out of sight. Moments later Blade saw the ghostly shapes of camouflaged parachutes deploying. The men were jumping alternately from the left and right sides of the gondolas, to keep them balanced.

The man to Blade's right was gone. Then the man opposite him followed. There was a hand on Blade's shoulder, and he heaved himself up on to the rim of the gondola. He was carrying sixty pounds of weapons and gear plus his chute. Then the hand was pushing into the small of his back, and he was stepping out into space.

As always, the fall until his chute opened seemed to go on forever. Once he was swaying under the canopy, Blade stopped worrying. It was an almost windless night at low altitude. He wouldn't be dragged helplessly across rough ground by a runaway parachute.

From somewhere off in the darkness came a long ghastly scream, dying away as the soldier with the faulty chute plunged to death. Blade swallowed and unslung his laser rifle. He might need to discourage a reception committee on the ground.

Nothing of the kind happened. Blade floated down to a standing-up landing in a meadow of long, sweet-smelling grass. By the time he'd got rid of his chute, three more men joined him. Two more came with a few minutes, one of them a female corporal from another platoon. Blade knew they were lucky not to be even more scattered and confused than this.

When it was clear that no one else was likely to show up soon, the corporal took command. She took her bearings and led her improvised squad off in what she hoped was the direction of the target village.

Blade rather hoped the corporal was wrong. If they did find the village, they might easily be hopelessly outnumbered by its defenders. Even if they weren't massacred, they would probably destroy the surprise and alert the Doimari advisers in time for them to flee. The Intelligence people would make life very difficult for anyone who wrecked their hopes of getting prisoners.

As they groped through the darkness, the ground underfoot began to slope sharply. Blade saw they were climbing down the side of a deep crater at least a hundred feet wide. It looked new, with only short grass and weeds growing on the sides. Blade stumbled over something hard, picked it up, and saw that it was a strip of worked metal. It was oddly light for its size and showed no signs of rust or corrosion.

Something fairly large had fallen or exploded here, not long ago. A sky-tug, either a Kaldakan scout or a Doimari one bringing supplies to the Tribes? Probably. But was there enough energy in the power cells of even the largest sky-tug to make a crater this big? Blade wished it were daylight. Maybe after the battle he could slip back here and get a closer—

An antigravity lifter whined overhead, the biggest Blade had seen. Out here tonight it had to be Doimari. Blade froze. So did the men behind and ahead of him. The man at the rear of the squad panicked and ran for the cover of some bushes. His movement drew the eye of someone in the lifter. A green laser beam speared through his body. He screamed. The corporal ran back to pull him under cover. A moment later the screaming man disintegrated as another laser beam detonated his grenades.

Blade hit the ground in time to escape. So did the two closest men. The corporal was caught by surprise and also by flying fragments. She grunted and sat down, then doubled up, kicking frantically. After a minute, blood trickled from her mouth and she lay still. Blade crawled to where the other survivors could hear him and whispered.

"We've got to go forward. If we pull back, we'll be on open ground and that thing'll laser us down. If we go forward, we'll be under cover."

"But the village must be alerted by now. They'll send out a patrol, and we won't have a chance."

68

"Not a good one," Blade admitted. "But better than if we try to outrun a laser beam."

The others couldn't deny an obvious truth, even when they heard it stated by a new recruit. It was one of those situations where the first man to make sense inherits the leadership.

The three soldiers crept through underbrush which quickly turned into heavy second-growth forest. They couldn't move through it as quietly as Blade would have liked, but he also knew they would be completely invisible even if somebody did hear them. Maybe they could go to ground here after all? Short of burning down the whole forest, the Tribesmen would only find them by luck. The rest of the company should catch up before that happened.

Before long they saw light through the trees. Finally they thinned out, and Blade crept forward for a closer look at the source of the light. Half a dozen Doimari were bustling around a stack of plastic boxes and wooden crates. Four were hauling them into a large earth and stone shelter, while two mounted guard. Beside the first shelter stood a second. On the roof was a large fish antenna and several radio aerials. Half a dozen timber-and-thatch Tribal huts were scattered around the other side of the clearing. Blade could make out the main village about a quarter of a mile farther down a winding path. Beside the pile of gear stood a lamp on a pole, shrouded so that it was almost invisible from above.

Blade's companions crawled up to join him. "We're in luck," he said. "We've stumbled on the ammo dump, they're not alert, and the village is a bit of a way off. If we hit them hard enough we can get the dump and a couple of prisoners before they wake up."

One man's eyes widened. "You're crazy! They couldn't have missed the shooting back there."

"No. But if the pilot didn't pass the word, they may not know what it was. They may think he was jumping at shadows."

"They still outnumber us—" began the other man, but the first private put a large hand on his shoulder.

"Shut up, Grudi, or you're gonna be the first casualty. I guess Voros is right. We got a better chance if we get 'em running around and falling over each other."

Blade grinned at his new ally. Private Ezarn was a huge ex-farmer, who took three men to handle him when he got drunk on payday. When he was sober in combat, he was worth half a platoon.

With only three men and no time to spare, Blade's tactics weren't fancy. He lasered out the light and, as darkness swallowed the clearing, threw four grenades as fast as he could pull the pins. The explosions started a fire in the pile of supplies, which lit up the clearing all over again. They also disabled most of the Doimari. Only two were on their feet when Blade and his comrades darted out into the clearing.

Ezarn and Grudi swung left. They were supposed to grenade the ammo dump before anyone inside could get the door shut. Blade shot one of the surviving Doimari, then swung right, heading for the huts and the path which led to the main village. He wanted to discourage the other Tribesmen from joining the fight for just a few minutes.

As he ran, he kept an eye out for the last of the Doimari. At last he saw the man darting from shadow to shadow, toward the shelter with the electronic array on the roof. Blade fired on the run, missed, and stopped for a better shot. This let the man make a flying leap through the shelter door and close it behind him. Blade swore. The man was probably going to either radio for help or blow up electronic equipment which Kaldakan Intelligence would be glad to have. He carefully aimed at the base of the dish antenna and fired, hoping to disable it.

He succeeded more thoroughly than he'd hoped. An electrical explosion flared blue-white, and pieces of half-melted metal showered down all over the clearing. Some landed in the dry thatch of the huts, which boomed into flames at once. Blade heard a woman scream from inside one hut. He headed for the cover of a tree on the far side of the clearing. It would let him cover the trail without being seen by the people who would certainly be swarming out of the huts in a minute.

Blade didn't move fast enough. A hut door flew open, and a young man dashed out. "You idiot!" he screamed at Blade. "Your fools with their fire weapons—" He broke off to look at one of the burning huts, turned pale, and screamed, "Klana!" Then he took a closer look at Blade, turned even paler, and drew his sword.

Blade slammed the butt of his rifle across the man's wrist. He howled, dropping the sword, but looked ready to leap on Blade with bare hands. His ears were twice normal size, pointed and hairy. "Get your wife and the others out of here!" Blade roared. "This isn't your fight. I won't hurt any of you unless I have to." He raised his rifle.

The young man gaped at Blade for a moment, his ears twitching, apparently wondering who was crazy here. Then he decided that he had nothing to lose and dashed into the nearest of the burning huts. He led out several people, one of them a woman even younger than himself with a baby at her breast. All the people had the same pointed, hairy ears, and they were coughing and rubbing their eyes. The baby was squalling loudly. The young man pointed off down the trail, and the people ran without a second warning or a backward glance.

The man stayed behind until the last of the people from the huts were gone. "I am Ikhnon, Chief of the Red Cots," he said to Blade, but then a laser beam from across the clearing nearly parted his hair. A second would have hit him, but just then the ammunition dump exploded with a deafening roar. The blast knocked Blade and the Tribesman chief flat and completely ruined the rifleman's aim. Twigs and birds' nests rained out of the tree; the young chief jumped up and ran. He was out of sight before the last rumble of the explosion died.

Blade turned to see Ezarn staggering toward him. He was half carrying Grudi in one hand and a heavy Doimari laser with a sack of power cells in the other. He was as black as a coal miner, but his teeth flashed white in a cheerful grin.

"Lots of stuff in there I hadn't seen before, but I couldn't figure how to use it. So I took a piece I knew. Figure we might have to do a little more fighting. That fellow you ran off, he'll be back with his friends."

"Maybe," said Blade. He looked down the trail, hoping to see signs the village was being evacuated. If the people got enough of a head start, the Kaldakans probably wouldn't bother chasing them. They'd have to abandon their livestock and everything else they couldn't snatch up in a hurry, but—

The Doimari lifter came whining in over the clearing. Blade and Ezarn dove for the nearest cover. Laser fire crackled wildly across the clearing, doing nothing except setting another hut on fire. Then the lifter settled down in the middle of the clearing. A hatch on top opened, and a man holding a laser rifle stuck his head out.

Before he could scan the clearing, Blade fired. The man slumped down, half out of the hatch. Blade and Ezarn dashed across the clearing, avoided the still-turning propellers of the lifter, and scrambled up on top of it. As they did, the door of the electronics shelter opened. A cloud of green smoke poured out, and so did several Doimari.

Blade and Ezarn flung themselves down among the Doimari. Blade was an expert at most forms of unarmed combat, and Ezarn was large and tough. In less than a minute all but one of the enemy sprawled unconscious on the ground. Ezarn shot the last one as he ran toward the village, while Blade cut his way through the locked side hatch of the lifter with his laser.

72

Inside he found the pilot struggling with the controls, trying to lift off but so panic-stricken he'd forgotten which buttons to push. The lifter was just beginning to lift when Blade clubbed him across the back of the skull with a rifle butt. He dropped back into his seat, and the lifter dropped back to the ground.

A moment later both Blade and Ezarn had to run for their lives as the Kaldakan sky-tug swooped in with its lasers blazing away. They barely got the unconscious Doimari under cover before the captured lifter blew up. Blade swore again.

The explosions woke up one of the Doimari. He looked at the flaming shambles around him and laughed hysterically. "You think you've won tonight, Kaldakan. You think you've won. But rest assured: we'll have our vengeance. Your city will look like this. Your own precious foolish Kaldak with no Sky Master to save youuuu—*unh!*" as Exarn knocked him unconscious again.

Blade and Ezarn looked at each other. "Wonder what he meant by that?" said the big man, rubbing his knuckles. "They maybe got some new kind of Fighting Machine?"

"I think he must have been hysterical," said Blade, sounding calmer than he felt. He remembered that crater with the metal shards and the electronic antennae on the hut. But if the Doimari were testing a secret weapon, why would they put their test station way out here in the Tribal lands, so far from their city and so vulnerable to enemy attack?

Blade was still trying to puzzle out the mystery when the rest of the paratroop company started to arrive, guided by the flames and the indignant radio messages from the sky-tug. It didn't help the commander's temper to discover that while he was trying to find his objective, the newest recruit in the company had won the battle almost single-handedly.

Chapter 10

If it had been up to the company commander, Blade probably wouldn't have received credit for his heroism. Grudi had been unconscious for most of the fight, and Ezarn had a bad reputation as a brawler and a drunk. They were the only Kaldakan witnesses.

Unfortunately for the commander, Ezarn had a much better reputation among his fellow soldiers than he did among the officers. They knew that when he called a new recruit "One-Man Army Voros," he should be listened to. So they listened, and in a day Blade's story was all over the company.

The Intelligence officers also heaped praise on Blade. Thanks to his quick work, they had several Doimari prisoners and a good description of the antennae. They were grateful and said so where higher-ranking officers than the company commander heard it.

Blade privately wished both Ezarn and the Intelligence officers would drop dead. He realized now that he'd reacted to stumbling on the Doimari as he usually did. He'd attacked, and so successfully that he'd made himself conspicuous again—the last thing he wanted to do in this Dimension!

Being an efficient and deadly fighting machine, it seemed, was a hard habit to break.

With the immediate area cleared of both Doimari and Tribesmen, a balloon train could land safely. It brought another company of the Fourth Battalion, with mortars and fresh ammunition. It took out the casualties, the Doimari prisoners, and the Intelligence officers. None of the prisoners would voluntarily answer a single question, so they were on their way to Kaldak and a session with the truth-seers.

The two companies moved toward their assigned position, leaving the mysterious crater behind before Blade could visit it in daylight. From conversations he overheard, there were other craters, but how many, how big, and where he couldn't tell. He didn't dare ask, either—that kind of curiosity was something sure to be noticed. He roundly cursed the fates again, for putting him in a situation where he had to spend so much time protecting his own secrets that he couldn't learn any of the secrets of this Dimension!

At least this was a Dimension he'd visited before, so it didn't have that many secrets. Also, the Kaldakans seemed able to take care of their enemies without needing his help. He wouldn't be hurting anything important by lurking as Private Voros until the time came for him to return Home.

As the two companies marched, scouts reported that the Tribesmen were abandoning their villages and scattering into the hills and forests. Sometimes the scouts or a sky-tug would burn a few houses in one of the abandoned villages, to keep the Tribesmen moving. Otherwise the two sides were leaving each other pretty much alone.

Blade wondered if both sides were saving their strength for a big fight? Or were the Tribesmen expecting that the Doimari would come to their rescue, or at least avenge them with the secret weapon— if there was one?

At last the two companies made contact with the main Kaldakan force. More Tribesmen had escaped than anyone liked, but some five hundred warriors were now trapped between the two Kaldakan forces. They had most of the livestock of several villages with them, so they could be a good prize. The

75

Kaldakans got ready to round up the herds and their herdsmen.

Blade's luck was going to hold in at least one thing. The enemy were all warriors. He still wouldn't have to shoot women and children.

"Open fire!"

Six stubby-barreled mortars went off in one long rolling crash. Six ten-pound shells went soaring over the top of the ridge to the west. A minute later the distant sound of explosions echoed from the valley. A signal lamp winked from a tree on the ridge line.

"Over and to the right," shouted the mortar commander. The mortar crews bent to make the adjustments, while the loaders stood ready with the next rounds.

Blade watched the activity with the eye of a professionally trained spectator. His platoon was assigned as security for the mortars. The nearest Tribesman was a good mile away, on the far side of the ridge and likely to stay there alive or dead. As the Fighting Machines advanced up the valley, they were supposed to drive the Tribesmen into the mortar fire.

It wasn't a bad plan, Blade knew. If it worked half as well as it was supposed to, the Tribesmen were finished, and no battle plan ever worked better than that. Now if the Tribesmen just did what they were supposed to . . .

The mortars crashed again; the echoes rolled up from beyond the ridge again. So did a growing cloud of smoke. The Kaldakan mortar shells weren't the best Blade had ever seen, but any weapon is good enough if it hits you.

Then a crash of a very different kind sounded, from behind Blade. Forty soldiers whirled around like puppets jerked by their strings. Something trailing bluish smoke hissed overhead. The smoke trail ended at the base of the observer's tree. Black smoke and flying branches rose in an ugly mushroom.

Another rocket went over, bursting close beside

the first. Blade saw a glimmer of green laser-light just below the rocket. So the Doimari had developed laser guidance systems for their rockets? And infiltrated a launcher team into the rear of the Kaldakans? They deserved credit for both their technology and their tactics.

Then Blade had to abandon his professional detachment. The platoon commander shouted, "Forward! Get those bastards!" then died with her mouth open as a third rocket hit the piled mortar ammunition. Fragments and whole shells flew in all directions, and one of them tore into the commander's chest. Another soldier had his head ripped off. His blood sprayed over Blade as he started to move out.

The attack got only a few steps before several lasers opened up, along with something like a grenade launcher. At least grenades which couldn't have been launched by hand were suddenly bursting among the Kaldakans.

That stopped the attack almost before it began. The platoon went to cover in the long dry grass of the meadow, moving only when grenade or laser-set fires burned too close. Some of the wounded couldn't move in time. Blade heard their desperate pleas for help, then their screams as they burned alive.

Blade ruthlessly closed his ears to the screams and watched the smoke from the fires thicken. Before long it would be thick enough to hide a moving man. Off to the left was a little ravine, running toward the enemy-held hill. Under cover of that ravine, a squad might get to within killing distance of the rocket launcher.

Blade looked at the men nearest him. Some were too stunned to move, others too badly wounded. He gritted his teeth. It looked as if he might have to do the work of a whole squad himself. He collected some extra grenades from two corpses and started crawling toward the ravine. At least this time he wouldn't have any witnesses to his work.

Halfway to the ravine the smoke started thinning.

77

Blade knew he'd be visible and vulnerable in another minute and gambled on speed. He leaped up and dashed for the bank of the ravine. As he reached it, the earth crumbled under his feet and dropped him ten feet to the shallow bed of a rocky stream.

Blade knew how to fall, so he wasn't hurt. Neither were his grenades. His laser rifle, however, was bent like a banana. Trying to fire it only produced a pathetic fizzing noise. Blade was annoyed with himself for being in such a hurry that he hadn't grabbed a spare rifle. Now he'd have to attack with grenades only, then pick up a rifle off a Doimari corpse. This would turn an already dangerous job into a real suicide party. However, the other choices were even worse. He could sit here until the Kaldakans won, when he would probably be court-martialed as a coward and possibly go under the truth-seer, or until the Doimari won, when they would kill or capture him.

At least he could be an anonymous hero this time. He rose to his feet, then jumped back as a large body hurtled down the side of the ravine. It trailed a cloud of dust and gravel, so Blade didn't recognize the man at once. Then the new arrival held out a laser rifle.

"Here, Voros. I brought two."

It was Ezarn. "What are *you* doing here?" snapped Blade.

"Coming with you," said Ezarn.

"You're crazy!"

"Not crazy like I'd be to lie there, let 'em chew me up. Or crazy like you going up there without no rifle." He dropped a fresh power cell into his own rifle. "Besides, you're lucky. Some of it'll rub off on me."

Blade wasn't so sure about that, but there was no time to argue. "All right. Follow me."

So Blade wound up being a public hero for the third time since his return to Kaldak.

He and Ezarn went up the ravine, then crawled to

78

within grenade-throwing distance of the Doimari without being detected. The Doimari were concentrating on doing as much damage to the apparently helpless Kaldakans below, and forgot about their flanks and rear. It was an old mistake, and just as fatal as usual when the grenades started bursting about their ears.

One of the grenades set off a rocket warhead, and it touched off several more rockets. When the smoke cleared away the rocket launcher was scrap metal and its crew mincemeat. Blade and Ezarn jumped up and waded into the survivors with their rifles, fists, and boots. Blade worked off a lot of anger and frustration on the surviving Doimari and Tribesmen.

When other Kaldakans finally joined them, twenty bodies were lying around. Another twenty Doimari and Tribesmen were running off in all directions, chased by the survivors of Blade's platoon. Blade himself was kneeling beside a badly wounded Doimari woman, apparently a technician, trying to give her first aid. She was too badly hurt to save, though, so he held her hand and pretended to be her father while she died.

Then he looked up to find the commander of the Fourth Battalion staring down at him. Blade realized he must be a fairly gruesome sight, his face black with smoke and dirt and most of his clothing soaked in blood.

"It's not *my* blood, sir," he said hastily.

The commander laughed. "Good. Then you'll live to get what you deserve. A promotion to Squad Leader at least, and whatever else High Commander Sidas thinks right."

"Sidas?" said Blade.

"That's right, you're the fellow who lost his memory." He explained who Sidas was and how Blade was going to be sent to Kaldak to be honored by the High Commander himself. When the battalion commander finished, he looked at Blade again.

"Meeting the High Commander doesn't make you nervous, does it?"

Not usually, would have been Blade's honest answer. *But when he's someone who might recognize me and expose the Dimension X secret, it's another matter.*

Aloud, he said, "No sir. Or at least not more than fighting the Doimari."

Chapter 11

Blade got a fresh uniform and boots and was told to tidy himself up to make a good appearance before Commander Sidas. He didn't have to shave off his beard; otherwise he would have seriously considered deserting. If Sidas recognized him or even got suspicious, he would almost certainly go under the truth-seer. As it was, Blade boarded the lifter for Kaldak with a positively piratical black beard. Few people will recognize a bearded man they've last seen clean-shaven thirty years ago. Blade was willing to gamble that Sidas wasn't one of them, in the hope of finding out more about what was going on in this Dimension. Even if nothing came of it for the Project, Blade was curious about what had come of his work.

A few friends in high places would also do Blade no harm in the eyes of Chyatho's friends.

The lifter spiraled down to a landing at what Blade christened "Kaldak Municipal Airport." It was six acres of rough asphalt, surrounded by hangars, wooden repair shops, and what had to be stables.

Teamsters led out a long cart drawn by twelve oxen. The lifter rose again, then settled onto the cart. The teamsters cracked their whips, and the oxen hauled the lifter off toward one of the hangars.

Blade shook his head as he watched them go. The combination of the far future and the Middle Ages in this Dimension still held a few surprises for him.

81

The airport was so close to the city that Blade's party walked the rest of the way. That was one advantage of antigravity—you didn't need to put the airports halfway into the next county to give the planes room for landing and taking off. Theoretically you could land a lifter right in the middle of the city. However, if the generators failed, lifters didn't glide. They came down like falling bricks. It was better to have them digging holes in farmers' fields than in the roofs of apartment buildings.

The road was crowded with traffic moving both ways in a fog of dust. Blade saw munfans—the kangaroo-like animals he had witnessed last visit— oxen, animals whose remote unmutated ancestors might have been something like horses, and lots of human porters. Every so often a Fighting Machine came whining along, making the dust worse and driving everyone to the edge of the road as it wavered past.

Halfway to the city they crossed a bridge over a canal which hadn't been there on Blade's first visit. He watched munfans and oxen pulling bargeloads of grain and timber along it. To the right of the bridge a gang of slaves was reinforcing the canal bank with slabs of stone. Blade caught their rank smell and heard the curses and whipcracks of the overseers. From the number of mutants among the slaves, they were probably Tribesmen.

Ezarn took Blade's preoccupation with all the sights and sounds of the new Kaldak for nervousness. "I know how you must be feelin'," he said cheerfully. "Me, too. Damned commanders can mess you up bad as Doimari, but you can't fight back. Leastways, if you shoot a commander, it makes a big fart."

Kaldak itself was still centered around the three towers Blade remembered, with eighteen streets radiating from them. Most of the buildings along the streets were the same, although cleaner. Some showed signs of repair with metal and cement instead of wood or stone.

A fringe of Newtec buildings surrounded the towers, rising to nearly half their height, One was still under construction—Blade saw a steam-powered crane hauling a metal beam aloft. Three of the eighteen streets were now public gardens and one was a market with shops and covered booths along both sides.

A fifth was now the parade ground for the army units quartered in Kaldak. Barracks, warehouses, and garages for the Fighting Machines jostled each other for room on either side. Blade's party went up this street to the headquarters of the High Commander in the tower at the far end.

Sidas had been a well-built, good-looking young warrior. He was still physically impressive, although his brown face was lined and his black hair was turning gray. He'd grown a bushy mustache and added a few pounds from sitting too long behind desks. He'd also added a shrewd, penetrating stare. The stare said plainly that he'd seen practically everything and it wasn't wise to try keeping secrets from him.

For someone in Blade's position, that stare was almost as unpleasant as the Doimari rocket barrage. He would have liked to think the stare was an act, but doubted it. Sidas had been one of the quickest learners among the warriors of Kaldak and must have stayed that way. Otherwise Kareena wouldn't have married him. Now he had all his natural intelligence plus thirty more years of experience. If anyone was likely to pierce the secret of Blade's identity, it would be Sidas.

Sidas walked up and down in front of Blade, Ezarn, and the other four men receiving medals today. He wore a plain green coverall, but his boots were leatherworkers' masterpieces, polished until they shone like glass. They also squeaked like angry mice with every step, until Blade was ready to grit his teeth.

Finally Sidas stopped in front of Blade. His eyes showed no sign of recognition as he pulled a small

83

box out of his belt pouch. "You know the Intelligence people want your hide now?" he said conversationally.

"No, sir. I didn't know."

"No reason for you to, either. It's secret, and stays that way." He fixed everyone in the room with a glare which promised death by slow torture for anyone with a loose tongue.

"We didn't learn anything from those Doimari you grabbed. Not an un-Lawful thing! Two of them didn't know anything, and the other died under the truthseer."

Some sort of hypnotic compulsion, probably, thought Blade. *The Doimari must really think their secret weapon is worth protecting.* Aloud, he said, "I'm sorry about that, sir."

"No way you could have known, Voros. No way at all. And that's what I've told the Intelligence people, and if they say anything more I'll throw them all into a pile of munfan dung! So you get the Star of Honor. Here." He handed the box to Blade. "For heroism, courage, and so on. You and your comrades know how well you did, and I'll leave the pretty words to someone else." He moved on to the next soldier.

Blade opened the box and saw a seven-pointed bronze star with "Honor" on it in Kaldakan script. He hung it around his neck, glad to have the High Commander's attention turned elsewhere for the moment. The less Sidas saw of him, the happier he would feel.

Right now Blade felt frustrated to the point of anger. He'd suspected that the Doimari might have some protection against interrogation. He'd even thought of mentioning the suspicion to the officers. But the company commander wouldn't have listened. The Intelligence people might have wondered how Private Voros came by this knowledge. Once again, he couldn't do half as good a job as he wanted to, because of the bloody bedamned Dimension X secret!

At last Sidas returned to Blade. "Voros," he said

abruptly. "You can go to the Commander's School if you want to. You've got a commander's head on your shoulders. You're a damned fine private, but you'll be better leading a platoon. Even a Company, maybe, before long, if the Tribesmen think Doimari weapons will let them go on fighting us. What do you say?"

"Sir, I'm honored. I accept."

"I was hoping you'd say that." They shook hands, and Sidas moved on again. Blade heard him offering equally generous rewards to the other men. One, who'd been badly wounded and was still on crutches, accepted early retirement on full pension. Another wanted a transfer to the Fighting Machine battalion of the City Regiment and got it. Ezarn asked for enough money so that his mother and sister could keep their farm.

Blade knew that he would be in the public eye as an officer cadet, still more as an officer leading troops. However, he was there already, thanks to his insisting on being a hero! Also, he'd passed the test with Sidas. Nobody else in Kaldak was as likely to recognize him. He wasn't safe by a long shot, but he could breathe a little easier.

He also had to admit that he wanted the greater freedom of action which would come with being an officer. As an officer, he wouldn't have to let Doimari take their secrets to the grave because he didn't dare speak up. And he *wanted* to help find out what the Doimari were up to. If he could help Kaldak without danger to the Dimension X secret, he would do it.

Ezarn came up to Blade outside Sidas's office and gave an exaggerated salute. "Sir, do I have permission to speak, *sir*?"

"Next time you ask my permission to speak, I won't give it." Blade growled. His voice was harsher than he'd intended. He'd rather looked forward to having Ezarn's rough comradeship while he was in Kaldak. Now he was going to be all alone again—

inevitable, perhaps, but even the inevitable can get a little wearing if it happens too often!

"All right. Thing is, this is the first time you and I can hit the taverns together. Also gonna be the last time, without some mother-raping Law-sucker kicking me for it. So let's get some of the boys together and move out."

"You won't have to drag me, Ezarn."

A long night of drinking sounded like a good idea. Blade wondered if Kaldakan liquor had improved any in the last thirty years. Even if it hadn't, it would let him forget about the Dimension X secret for a few hours.

Chapter 12

The soldiers' tavern was like others Blade had seen in many Dimensions. It was overcrowded, hot, noisy, and smoky. Here in Kaldak the smoke came from something burned in brass pots hung from the ceiling on chains. To Blade it smelled like old rubber tires, but the Kaldakans didn't seem to mind it. He wondered if it was a narcotic, an aphrodisiac, or simply intended to make people get drunk faster so they wouldn't have to go on smelling it!

The brass pots hung so low that Blade had to duck his head to get under most of them. Many of the Kaldakans were short enough not to have this problem, but Ezarn had already knocked himself out. Now he lay snoring quietly in one corner. A comrade mounted guard over him, to keep people from robbing, trampling, or vomiting on him.

Blade had put down several large jugs of beer. The dark-haired girl on his lap kept trying to make him drink hard liquor. He kept refusing. Kaldakan liquor was bad enough straight. Taking it on top of beer—well, he didn't want to show up for his first day at the Commander's School with a history-making hangover.

After a while the girl started to plaster herself against Blade. She was pleasantly curved and felt warm and comfortable against him. It helped that her blouse was now open and her skirt hiked up to mid-thigh, and she wasn't wearing any underclothes.

As her blouse slipped down off her shoulders, Blade saw tattoos on the upper slopes of both breasts. He prodded them with a forefinger.

"Tribe?" he said.

The girl wouldn't meet his eyes. He put a hand under her chin and lifted her head gently until she did. "Yes," she said finally. "I was taken when I was fourteen. The son of the farmer who bought me freed me when I was twenty. But what could I do with the freedom, except come here?" Blade caught the note of desperate defiance in her voice. She'd swallowed her pride enough to let her earn a living as a tavern whore, but it was still there.

Blade decided to make the Tribal girl's evening profitable and his own a little more enjoyable. He ran a hand up her leg to the edge of her skirt. When she didn't protest he ran it up farther. As he stroked the inside of her thigh, she opened his shirt and ran her hand over his bare chest.

"Old scars," she murmured. "Not from the battle we've all heard about. Where did you get them, Voros?"

"I wish I knew," he said. "I know I was a soldier, because I remember everything about how to fight. I don't remember where I fought."

"Hmmmm," she said, laying her lips against Blade's bare skin. "Couldn't you have them truth-see you?"

"I suppose I could," said Blade, more casually than he felt. "But what if something happened to me to make me lose my memory? Something so horrible that I had to forget it or go mad? Would I gain anything by remembering it now?"

"I understand," the girl murmured. "If I could forget the night they took our village . . ."

A gong sounded from the end of the room. "Fill up, fill up, my friends," shouted the tavern owner. "Fill up, and do justice to Rokhana, the unique, wonderful, exquisite Rokhana. You can't see any of her anywhere else but you can see all of her here tonight and every night at the Defenders' Rest!"

88

He repeated this announcement several times in a whiskey baritone, beating the gong all the while. The tavern girls circulated with bottles and pitchers, filling everybody's cups and glasses, dancing out of the way of any man who grabbed at them. Some didn't—they'd "brought their own" in the form of a female comrade. Blade saw two of the women soldiers leading their men toward the stairs to the upper floors of the tavern. Up there were forty or so "sleeping rooms"; sometimes they really were used for sleeping.

The tavern owner went on beating the gong until Blade felt a strong desire to stuff the padded stick he was using down his gullet. A drummer and a horn player came out from behind the bar and sat under the gong. The drummer started pounding a steady beat in time with the gong, while the horn player tuned his instrument. At least Blade supposed he was tuning it; one dying-cow blast sounded very much like another.

Finally the band was ready. At a signal from the tavern keeper the girls pulled back half a dozen tables to make a clear space in the middle of the floor. The horn player blew such a long blast that Blade wondered where he got the breath for it. Then the curtain over the door to the stairs flew aside and the long-awaited Rokhana pranced into the room.

She was a tall, well-built blonde, who moved in a way both erotic and graceful at the same time. Everything she wore was in a shade of green which went well with her hair—cloak, hat, jacket, blouse under the jacket, calf-length skirt, and boots so floppy Blade wondered how she was going to dance in them.

A moment later, Blade found out. Rokhana simply swayed and wiggled in time to the musicians' beat where she stood. With most women that would have been unimaginative or even boring. With Rokhana it was exciting by itself, and gave promise of better things to come.

After a minute she undid the clasps of her cloak and shrugged it free of first one shoulder, then the other. She caught it before it hit the floor, without missing a beat. Then, still in time with the musicians, she threw it accurately onto the sleeping Ezarn. Blade joined in the roar of laughter.

The hat followed. It passed so close to Blade that he could have caught it without the girl on his lap. Then Rokhana kicked high twice, sending her boots sailing over the bar. Somehow she managed the high kicks without showing anyone what she wore under the skirt. She did show off long, elegant legs. Laughter turned into bawdy shouts.

Now Rokhana could move freely about the floor. Her bare feet seemed to twinkle—or was it the beer and the smoke making Blade's vision uncertain? All he knew was that suddenly the jacket was flying toward him, draping itself over the girl on his lap. There was something ugly in the laughter this time. Blade thought he heard the girl curse in her Tribal tongue.

By the time Blade got his girl untangled, Rokhana was undoing her blouse a button at a time. It didn't really matter that much, since she was wearing something under it. The cheers and the handclapping still swelled until they began to drown out the musicians. The musicians played louder, and the din hammered at Blade's ears.

Rokhana's blouse had buttons at the wrists as well as down the front. She undid the wrist buttons with her teeth, while holding the free hand modestly in front of her gaping blouse. Then she started wriggling her shoulders and torso. Slowly the blouse slid down, while an inch at a time she pulled it out of the waist of her skirt. She had to stand still while she was doing this, but nobody would have been watching her feet in any case.

Rokhana's upper body seemed to move in three

directions at once, and suddenly the blouse was on the floor. Under it she wore a sort of halter top, which did nothing to hide the shape of her breasts or much to restrain their movement. For a moment one long-fingered hand rested lightly over a nipple. Then Rokhana was on the move again. So was her skirt—down her hips.

Things began to flow together now for Blade. He suspected he was actually calmer than most of the men in the tavern. All around he heard heavy breathing, as if the soldiers had run hard or lifted heavy weights. In one corner a man and a woman stood locked so close together he couldn't tell if they were actually making love or not.

Rokhana stepped out of her long skirt and pranced freely in a short skirt and the halter. Somehow her hair had come undone, and as her dancing grew wilder it tossed like a golden mane around her head. It caressed her bare freckled shoulders, and Blade felt his hands itching to do the same. He also felt the girl on his lap moving, and her hand between his legs. The raw sex in the air of the tavern was getting to everyone.

Half a dozen men stood up to catch Rokhana's short skirt when she tore it off. For a moment it looked as if they would fight for it, then they all drew back. They must have known that a brawl would end the striptease before it reached its climax. They would sit on an anthill or fight Tribesmen bare-handed before they would do that. Not when Rokhana was now parading in the halter and shorts so short they hardly covered more than a G-string. . . . Blade had to remind himself to breathe.

He wouldn't have believed that the music could get louder, but it did. So did the stamping and clapping. Several more couples were now in secluded corners. There was no doubt about what some of them were doing. Blade's eyes lingered on one couple just long enough to miss the moment when Rokhana's halter top came off. From the wolfpack

91

howl all around him, he still knew what to expect when he looked back at the woman.

Her breasts would have been too large for any woman smaller or less broad-shouldered. On her they were just right. Their large nipples were now fully erect. She writhed in place, so that each breast seemed to move independently. Meanwhile her hand crept tantalizingly down one smooth flank to the front of her shorts. The cheering began to fade, because everyone was now too dry-throated.

One button at the front of the shorts. Two. Three. Rokhana flowed down onto the floor until she was lying on her back. Now she writhed as if she felt a lover already deep inside her. Suddenly she threw her legs and pelvis clear of the floor. At the same time she snatched the shorts down to her knees. As if she had springs in her legs, she bounced to her feet, kicked high and sent the shorts flying. Everyone was too paralyzed to move, as she stood stark naked in the middle of the room. The musicians stopped playing. Blade had never heard such a complete silence in a room with so many people in it.

Blade raised his head, and Rokhana's wide blue eyes met his. A little shudder went through her, starting at the ankles and working up. It made her breasts sway. Then she was walking toward him, suddenly almost awkward, feeling her way as if she were walking over stony ground. The proud lust-goddess was gone, and in her place a woman who desperately wanted the hero of the hour but was afraid of being rejected.

She came up to Blade and leaned over him until her nipples were at the level of his eyes. She smiled. He smiled back. She laid a hand on his shoulder. He reached up and patted her on one hip.

Then the Tribal girl in Blade's lap turned around and punched Rokhana hard in the stomach.

The blow caught Rokhana off-balance. She let out a *whuff* and staggered backward. She would have gone down if she hadn't stumbled over someone's outstretched foot and landed in his lap. The soldier laughed and threw an arm around her waist. She cursed, twisted around, and slapped his face. Before he could reach for her again, she was on her feet, striding back toward Blade and the Tribal girl. She no longer looked in the least vulnerable. Instead she looked ready for murder.

The Tribal girl slid off Blade's lap and got ready to defend herself. She looked frightened half out of her wits at her own boldness, but determined to die rather than beg for the mercy Rokhana probably wouldn't show. In fact, it was the girl who launched herself at the other woman.

They grappled, too much in deadly earnest to waste time screaming or pulling hair. The girl tried to punch Rokhana in the stomach again. Rokhana aimed a punch at the girl's breast. It connected. She gasped at the pain but closed with her opponent, trying to grapple again. That would take away some of the advantage Rokhana's longer reach gave her.

Rokhana danced out of range and kicked at the girl's groin. The girl rode the blow and gripped Rokhana's ankle, but Rokhana twisted free before the girl could throw her. As she did, she missed her footing and went down. Before she could get up, the girl was on top of her. Her sturdy legs clamped around Rokhana's waist and her hands felt for the blonde woman's throat. An animal roar went up as the girl started to squeeze. Blade looked at the tavern keeper, hoping to see him ready to interfere. Instead the man was staring at the fight with glazed eyes, licking his lips as the girl's fingers tightened.

Rokhana kicked and clawed at the girl. Her nails shredded the girl's blouse and left bloody streaks down her bare back, but didn't break her grip. Then Rokhana's desperately searching eyes fell on a heavy metal beer pitcher lying on the floor just within reach. She grabbed it and smashed it across the girl's forehead. The girl gave a little whimper but held on. Rokhana's lips were beginning to turn blue.

Then she somehow found the strength to swing the pitcher again. It crashed against the girl's temple. This time her grip broke, and she toppled sideways. She sprawled on the floor, bare to the waist and nearly as exposed below, while Rokhana gasped for air.

Then the blonde was on her feet again, swaying, stumbling, ignoring the hands which darted out to pinch and feel her sweating flesh. She stood over the half-conscious Tribal girl and kicked her in the stomach. The crowd roared. Rokhana kicked again, harder.

Blade stood up. Whatever the Tribal girl might deserve, he wasn't going to sit quietly by and let her be murdered. Still less was he going to cheer it on. He moved out onto the floor so fast he was behind Rokhana before anyone noticed. She'd just kicked again when he threw both arms around her and pulled her back out of reach of the girl.

For a moment Rokhana struggled, until Blade found himself gripping her breasts. Then she stopped struggling and turned to face him. He almost recoiled from the look in her eyes. She was so near the edge of madness with anger and arousal that she'd be quite happy if he took her here, now, on the floor in front of everybody. The howl from all around them told Blade other men saw the same thing.

Instead he put one arm under her thighs and another under the small of her back and lifted her. Ignoring the girl and the shouts, he carried her to the stairway door. He kicked the door shut behind them, then carried Rokhana up the stairs to the nearest unoccupied room with a bed.

The bed was narrow and rickety and the room smelled of stale beer and unwashed bodies, but it didn't matter. Neither of them could have waited long enough to find anything better.

In the darkness Blade felt Rokhana stretch and press herself against him. Even now, she felt incredibly good.

94

He cupped a breast and stroked her hair with the other hand. She didn't respond as she had before. After a moment he said, "You're thinking about the Tribal girl."

He heard a little gasp. "Are you a truth-seeing wizard, like the Sky Master Blade?"

"No. But if I'd just been nearly strangled by someone, I might be thinking about them, too."

"I was. At first I thought I would see that she was tried. That would mean death, for her."

"She's a free woman."

"Her blood is of the Tribes. The Law can be bent for such. And I know how to bend judges, if it is needed." She put her hand on Blade in the appropriate place.

"Don't try to bend that, or you'll have *my* hands on your neck."

"I'll gladly have your hands on me anywhere."

"Prove it."

She did, and so thoroughly it was quite a while before they were talking again. "You say you thought you would have the girl tried?" asked Blade. "What now?"

"If her skull isn't cracked and her guts bleeding, it won't be because I didn't try. She'll lose her job and not find it easy to get another in Kaldak. If she has to go back to the farms, that will be enough vengeance for me."

"You're being rather easy on someone who tried to kill you."

"She won't get a second chance, believe me, For now, I do as the Sky Master Blade and his consort the Blessed Kareena taught us. She sought peace with the Doimari, even after what she suffered at their hands. It was not her fault that they would not see reason."

Blade couldn't recall what he'd said when he was Sky Master which might be the basis for this "teaching," but was still glad. His influence had reached out across thirty years and saved an ex-slave girl from an ugly death. It was an oddly satisfying feeling.

Then Rokhana was moving again, and he felt something just as satisfying in a different way. She rolled over on top of him, her lips traced a path down his throat, chest, and belly, then closed hungrily on his shaft. He sank his fingers into her hair to hold her in position while she worked. . . .

Blade didn't appear at the Commander's School next morning with a hangover, but he was very short of sleep.

Chapter 13

"Commander's School Company—attention!"

Blade slammed his booted heels together with a smart thump. On either side of him, a hundred and fifty men and women did the same thing.

"Flag Guard—forward!"

Blade took three steps forward, then to the right to close up with the other members of the squad. Membership in the Flag Guard was a considerable honor for a Commander Cadet. You needed a spotless record, high grades, and a natural talent for close-order drill. Or at least they thought it was "natural talent" in Blade's case. He'd fitted in so well at the Commander's School that he sometimes wondered if anyone would believe the truth if he told them.

He still wasn't tempted to do it, though.

Gravel crunched under booted feet to his left as the inspection party made its way along the ranks of the Company. Blade had to keep his eyes rigidly forward, but they walked slowly enough so that he got a good long look at them.

Sidas led, a sash across his broad chest but otherwise looking much the same as he had in his office. Some of the high-ranking Kaldakans went in for fancy uniforms, but not Sidas.

He was escorting Councilor Geyrna. She would be in her mid-forties now, and her red hair was turning gray. She was still a handsome woman, with the full bosom and ready smile Blade remembered in the fifteen year old merchant's daughter who'd loved the chief's son. He wondered what might have happened between her and Bairam, to make her divorce him and stay in Kaldak, rather than share his exile. Had he played around a little too freely with other women? That would be like the man, Blade thought.

Geyrna had her own personal staff, headed by a striking dark-haired woman. She must have been close to six feet tall, with a magnificent figure, although her face was too long and her nose too big for classic beauty. She carried herself like a thoroughbred mare. Blade had to force himself not to stare.

Then the inspection party was past, and the drillmaster was shouting, "Company—right face! Flag Guard—lead!" As the Flag Guard took their position at the head of the company, the band struck up, and the drillmaster gave his final order.

"Forward march!"

The company passed in review. Blade kept perfect step, and the angle of his laser rifle never varied by a single millimeter. He still could not quite get the dark-haired woman out of his mind. He hadn't seen her before in this Dimension, he was sure. Did she remind him of someone he'd known elsewhere? Perhaps—there'd been so many women.

After the ceremonies, the School Commander announced an unexpected half-day's holiday. Blade was taking a shower and wondering what to do with the free time when one of his comrades stuck his head into the bathroom.

"Huh, Voros. You free tonight?"

"So far, Kabo. Why?"

"Good. Commander Baliza's inviting a few of us to dinner in her quarters."

"Baliza?"

Kabo grinned. "The chief of Councilor Geyrna's staff. Remember her?" His hands outlined a well-built woman.

"Now I do. Dinner, you say?"

Kabo leered. "Don't get your hopes or anything else up, Voros. She's cast-iron all the way through and all the way up and down. Save your balls for women who'll give them back when they're through."

Blade tried to look innocent. "I won't do anything without orders."

Kabo laughed. "Good. If the evening breaks up early, knock on my door. We can go into town and visit the Golden Munfan. They say the dancers there are even better than Rokhana."

"I'll believe that when I see it."

Baliza's dinner party started off rather bleakly. Blade felt rather like a small boy at a fancy tea party, watched over by a particularly grim nurse. From the look on the faces around him, he wasn't the only one. Baliza sat at the head of the table, her face so expressionless that it was hard to think of her as alive, let alone a woman. She wore civilian clothes cut even more severely than her uniform, and her hair was bound up tightly on top of her head. It made her look positively horse-faced. At least the food and drink were good, and Blade was hungry enough to let that make up for the frigid atmosphere.

Over desert Baliza began to relax, drawing out each of the cadets on what he or she had done before joining the army. She saved Blade for last, so he was able to organize his lies about a loss of memory even better than usual. So why did he get the feeling afterward that she was skeptical? It was a vague feeling, not much he could really put his finger on, rather like the feeling that he'd seen Baliza or someone like her before.

Added together, the two vague feelings gave him one which wasn't vague at all. He wanted to see as little of Baliza as he could manage, because he didn't want her to see much of him. He'd heard that Geyrna carried more weight on the Council of Nine than any other three members put together. If that was so, the suspicions of anyone who had Geyrna's ear could be much more dangerous to Blade than even High Commander Sidas's.

When they got up from the table, Blade headed for the balcony outside. There he might stay out of Baliza's sight for the rest of the evening. Even if she came out on the balcony, the light there was poor. Baliza's quarters were on the third floor, and the balcony faced a lightless garden.

Blade was noticing that the garden would provide excellent cover when he heard footsteps behind him. They sounded almost like Baliza's usual brisk stride, but not quite. He turned. There was enough light to show him that she now wore soft sandals instead of boots. She'd also made a few other changes. She wore a knee-length skirt and a snug top which left her shoulders bare. Blade couldn't help staring at her fine breasts outlined under the cloth, and her well-formed bare legs.

Baliza stepped closer. Somehow Blade wasn't surprised to discover that she was now wearing perfume.

"Hello, commander," said Blade, feeling that he ought to do more than stand and wait for her to make her move. "Would you like to go down and walk in the garden?"

"Does it remind you of home?" she said with a smile.

"It reminds me of—somewhere I've been before," he said. "Whether that place was my home or not, I don't . . . know."

"Do you think you ever will?"

"I can't say. I know that I'm quite happy where I am now. Happy enough not to spend much time worrying about the past." He hoped that would turn her aside from this line of talk before the matter of the truth-seer came up.

He was disappointed. "Perhaps you are happy enough. Certainly you ought to be. You have done well for Kaldak and for yourself. Perhaps you will do even better in time. But what of those you may have

100

left behind, in the darkness where your memory does not go?"

Blade hid his uneasiness. "I do not know that there are any such people."

"So you say."

Blade pretended to be indignant. "I hope you are not calling me a liar, commander. Even from you, I will not take that willingly."

"I do not call you a liar." She stepped closer to him. "I believe you are telling the truth, as you know it. But how much of it can you be sure that you know?"

"Not very much."

She was now so close that he could have taken her in his arms if he'd wanted to. Certainly she seemed ready for it. To Blade's heightened senses, the smell of her perfume and her arousal together was over-powering.

"Then can you be sure there is no woman, no child left alone in a place you have forgotten, thinking you are dead, grieving for you? *Can you?*" She emphasized her words further by pressing herself against his chest. Her hair was unbound and it whispered softly as she moved her head.

Blade decided to yield to the inevitable. If he exhausted her with lovemaking, it *might* turn her aside from this rather alarming line of questioning she was pursuing. He slipped a hand inside the waist of her skirt. It fell on the curve of bare buttocks. She was wearing nothing under the skirt.

She sighed with obvious pleasure at the feel of his hand on her. "I am sorry. Perhaps I am asking more of you than you can give. I hope not, though," She giggled, then was serious again. "It is just that I feel sorry for anyone you may have left behind. My mother was killed when I was nine. I wanted for nothing, because I was the Sky Master Blade's daughter, but—"

Blade tried to say something, and realized that it

101

had come out a wordless croak. He jerked his hand away from Baliza.

The Sky Master Blade's daughter. *His own daughter?* But—

"Your mother was—?" he managed to get out.

"Kareena, daughter of Peython. As I said, I wanted for nothing. But those who gave me everything else could not give me back my mother, and my father had returned to the sky, this we knew. So I know what it is to be alone. I will not be alone tonight, though. I—Voros, what is wrong?"

Blade was as close to being completely speechless as he'd ever been in his life. The narrowness of the margin by which he'd avoided committing incest with his own daughter did *not* make for a clear mind or a nimble tongue. Since he doubted he could say anything sensible, he said nothing.

That was a mistake. Baliza seemed to take his silence as a sign he was too aroused to speak. That wasn't entirely wrong. Blade's mind was digesting the fact that Baliza was his daughter; his body was still reacting to her as a desirable woman. He had the feeling that in another moment she would notice this fact, and then the fat would really be in the fire!

He took a step backward. Another mistake. She laughed. "Are you afraid you've lost interest, Voros? Well, I'll see what I can do to bring it back." With impossibly swift movements she stripped off her upper garment. Her hard-nippled breasts had no sag in them anywhere. They would have aroused a dead man—or Richard Blade, if they'd belonged to any other woman in any Dimension. Instead he took another step backward.

Baliza took two steps to his one and pressed herself against him. At the same time she caught up one of his hands and drew it hard against one breast. Blade's fingers twitched involuntarily. Baliza broke into a giggle as she felt his erection against her.

"So. You haven't lost interest after all. Neither have I." She pressed harder, until he could feel her
102

nipples through his shirt. She threw one arm around him, and with her other hand fumbled at the catch of her skirt.

In another moment she would be completely naked, and that thought was the end of the matter for Blade.

If the stakes had been higher, he might have let her go ahead. If he would have been saving lives or the Dimension X secret by committing incest, he would probably have done so. Blade's conscience was not that tender, particularly when the daughter in question was a grown woman, obviously no virgin, and quite ignorant of who it was that she was so expertly seducing.

However, in the present situation there wasn't enough at stake. Blade's scruples took over. He jumped back, opening a gap of several feet between him and Baliza. As her skirt slipped off, he put both hands on the balcony railing. She stepped forward, naked and ready, and he vaulted over the railing and dropped into the garden.

Bushes under the balcony broke his fall. They also absorbed the flower pot Baliza threw after him. They did nothing to muffle the curses she shrieked after him.

The old proposition that "Hell hath no fury like a woman scorned" was receiving new proof tonight.

Baliza's curses followed Blade as he hurried through the garden. Halfway to the back wall, he nearly stumbled over two of his comrades from the dinner party. They were entwined on the ground, busily putting a moonlit night and a secluded garden to a traditional use. He reached the back wall and wasted no time looking for a gate. Five minutes after leaving Baliza's embrace, Blade was out in a back street, heading back toward the barracks. He would have run, but he didn't want to attract attention. Also, he wanted to give himself a little time to think about what to do next.

The simplest and most obvious course was to just

keep moving, out of Kaldak and into the wilderness where he could hide until the time came to return to Home Dimension. Apart from his dislike of simply running away from trouble, Blade decided that would be too drastic for now.

Once her anger cooled, Baliza might be embarrassed by the night's incident. In fact, she might be too embarrassed to say anything, let alone retaliate. She might owe some of her rank to being the Sky Master's daughter, but she didn't sound like a complete idiot!

If Baliza kept her mouth shut, nothing would happen to Blade. But if in the meantime he'd disappeared, it wouldn't matter what Baliza said. Suspicion would be aroused, the manhunt would be on, and his position would be precarious, to say the least. So would the position of the Dimension X secret.

The best thing was to go back to the barracks as if nothing had happened. Baliza could hardly take any action tonight. If she made her move tomorrow, he would be more likely to get advance warning of it in the barracks, among his comrades. He could also keep weapons and food ready to hand in case he had to flee, instead of leaving Kaldak with nothing but the clothes he stood up in.

Blade returned to the barracks just as Kabo was leaving for his night on the town. Unable to think of any better way of making things look normal, Blade let himself be talked into joining the party.

He never did find out if the dancers at the Golden Munfan were better than Rokhana, though. He wasn't calm enough to pay full attention to the first one, and though the second one was definitely not as good as Rokhana, after her act she came over and sat on his lap. One thing led to another, he missed all the rest of the dances, and it was nearly dawn when he got back to the barracks.

Chapter 14

Blade's day was so normal that he began to hope he'd guessed right. Baliza wanted the whole night's episode swept under the rug. He certainly would have, in her place.

He was coming off the firing range when Kabo stopped him. "Voros, the School Commander wants you in his quarters." Kabo both looked and sounded unhappy.

"Any idea what he wants?"

Kabo looked even more unhappy. "Yes, but—well, will you forgive me if I say I don't want to get my dong caught in the gears along with yours?"

Blade grinned. "If it's about how I spent last night—or rather, *didn't* spend part of it, I don't blame you. Don't worry. The ax is still a long way from my neck. It shouldn't be too hard to jump aside."

Kabo made a gesture for averting bad luck. "I hope you're right."

So did Blade. He wasn't as optimistic as he'd tried to sound as he walked to the Commander's quarters. If Baliza was really going to make a fuss, he would need fast footwork and a *very* nimble tongue.

The School Commander was sitting behind his desk, wearing dusty fatigues and a bad-tempered expression. Blade saluted.

"Good evening, sir."

"What's good about it? Never mind. You've put

your foot in it. Now tell me how you're going to get it out."

The explanation was brief and to the point. Baliza was charging him with attempted rape. He'd fled after she threatened to scream, but—

"What did you say, Voros?"

"Nothing, sir." *Or at least nothing printable.*

The commander went on. Actual rape meant mandatory truth-seeing *and* confinement in the meantime. Attempted rape meant a choice of confinement *or* truth-seeing.

"If I was in your position, I'd go under the truth-seer. I won't call Baliza a liar, but I'd like to get your story, too. Then it's possible we might get Baliza under the truth-seer as well. Not likely—she's the Sky Master's daughter, even if she did take Bairam's side when he was thrown off the Council. However, Geyrna has forgiven her, so no one dares not listen to her even if they don't like her. A lot don't like her, though, and if your story doesn't support hers—"

The Commander rambled on for a while, repeating things Blade understood the first time. He would have been impatient, but obviously the Commander was trying to talk out his own nervousness over the situation.

Blade saw two choices. He could give his oath to go under the truth-seer, then do it within a day or two at most. Or he could go to prison, and wait in a cell for his trial. If he did the second, he wouldn't be able to leave Kaldak without escaping from prison. That would attract attention, to say the least. Also, he might wind up under the truth-seer anyway—and he had to avoid that at all costs.

The Dimension X secret really had been at stake last night, but he hadn't realized it. Oh, well, hindsight was always twenty-twenty. What to do now?

Swear an oath to go under the truth-seer, then *run.* Kaldak was now much too hot to hold him.

But—run where?

He would be safe enough in the wilderness which

still covered much of this Dimension. Uncomfortable, but safe. He would be slightly more comfortable but somewhat less safe among the Tribes, who were in any case a long way off. The same thing went for Monitor Bekror and his estate. The Monitor was surly and independent-minded toward Kaldak. He still might not be ready to hide a fugitive accused by the Sky Master's own daughter.

That left Doimar. The border wasn't far, nor was it that heavily patrolled—at least on the Kaldakan side. If Blade pretended to be a defector from Kaldak, he might learn a few of Doimar's secrets. He might not learn enough to wreck Doimar's war plans, as he had last time. He might not even learn enough to win back his position in Kaldak—which didn't really matter, since he wasn't going to be in this Dimension forever. He could still leave the information in safe hands before he returned Home.

In Doimar, he would be out of reach of Baliza and the truth-seers. The rival city had no such devices. They were said to have telepaths, but that was only a rumor and Blade was willing to take his chances with them. He'd resisted the telepathy of the Wizard of Rentoro, whose mind had been powerful enough to transport him from Renaissance Italy into Dimension X.

Blade became aware that the School Commander was looking expectantly at him.

"Well?"

"Sorry, sir. I'll go under the truth-seer."

"And you give your word of honor not to leave Kaldak before then?"

"Yes, sir." He'd told larger lies to protect smaller secrets.

"Very good. Dismissed—and good luck."

"Thank you, sir."

Shortly after midnight, Blade left Kaldak. A week later, he was across the border into Doimar.

A week after that, he was in prison in a research laboratory far from the city, waiting to be used as an experimental subject.

Blade stared at the wall and tried to shut the moans of the dying woman in the far corner of the cell out of his mind.

The cracks on the wall stared back.

This was one of the times when the cracks took the shape of a gigantic rabbit with a single huge eye set between its ears. If Blade concentrated on this rabbit long enough, it began to seem about to say something to him.

If he'd thought it would tell him how to get out of here, he would have listened. However, it hadn't said anything yet. He'd learned more from the surly guards and even from the woman, although she'd been half-mad with pain and fever the first day she was in the cell with Blade.

After a while Blade knelt beside the woman's sodden pallet and sponged her off again. She looked like a concentration camp victim, her naked body gaunt and covered with the oozing sores of the fever with which she'd been infected.

When he'd finished sponging her, Blade dropped the foul-smelling cloth into the waste can and held a cup of water to her lips. She swallowed it, more by reflex than anything else, and gripped Blade's free hand in both of hers. She still had the strength to grip painfully hard. Blade put down the cup and let her hold on until suddenly she was slimy with sweat again. The attack of fever was breaking.

At last the woman turned on her side with a little whimper and fell peacefully asleep. Blade sat cross-legged beside the pallet and gritted his teeth. He didn't know the woman's name, where she came from or why she'd been sent here. She might even be a criminal. He still knew that if he had to go on much longer watching her die by inches, he was going to go berserk. He would start tearing guards apart

108

with his bare hands, killing them until he was killed himself.

That would be foolish, of course.

The guards were an unpleasant lot, but hardly essential to Doimar's war effort. He could kill a hundred of them without setting back Doimar's plan of conquest by a single day. Better to wait until he could take out a few of the key Seekers—those who made up Doimar's scientific elite.

However, even if he killed Seekers, he would die here in Doimar. What he'd learned would die with him. He might gain Kaldak some time, but if they didn't learn the danger they faced, would they be able to put it to good use?

Blade doubted it. Kaldak was nearly a democracy; Doimar was nearly a dictatorship. A democracy can catch up with a dictatorship in war if it has the time. If Blade's theory about Doimar's plans was correct, Kaldak wouldn't have the time.

In plain English, the Doimari were planning to bombard Kaldak with ballistic missiles, carrying warheads loaded with deadly germs. Possibly other things as well (nerve gas, nuclear weapons, radioactive dust?), but germs for certain.

The Doimari wouldn't have been at all happy to find out how easily Blade learned their secret. The night they brought him to the research complex, he'd seen an unmistakable gantry crane on the horizon. He'd heard the equally unmistakable sound of large rockets being fired several times. (And now he understood the secret of the Doimari base he'd surprised. It was a ranging and tracking station for the missiles; the craters around it were from test missiles or warheads.)

Blade had been brought to this cell in the research complex to act as a gunea pig in the test for new strains of deadly germs. He found this out from the guards who'd brought the woman in and had wondered out loud if she would infect him.

"Probably," said one. "Does it matter?"

"I don't bet either way. I've heard they're ready with Culture S, so they may not need any more tests."

"Maybe. But this one—he looks like a fighter. Suppose they want to find out how long he can handle a weapon with S in him? That's something could mean your arse and mine when the Day comes."

"All right. But we'd better shout the first thing he shows any sores."

"*He'll* shout loud enough. You ever heard anyone in first stage?"

"No."

"You don't want to, either."

The guards went out, and the last piece of the Doimari puzzle fell into place for Blade.

Although Blade's deductions would have surprised the Doimari, they wouldn't have surprised J. He knew that Blade was an exceptionally keen observer, even by the standards of a profession whose members had to be rather sharper than the average if they were to live long enough to draw their pensions or even justify much of their not too generous salaries. Blade treasured a remark passed on to him by a friend who'd overheard J say, "Richard is in a class by himself awake. He's fairly good sound asleep. And frankly, I wouldn't care to reveal any secrets in the same room as his corpse."

Unfortunately the Doimari weren't being hospitable to "defectors" from Kaldak. Of course Blade couldn't have known that. He'd had to run, and even though getting captured and put into the Doimari research complex hadn't kept him from figuring out what they were up to, it would probably keep him from doing any vital damage. It would almost certainly keep him from getting a warning to Kaldak. That could make his trip just as useless as if he'd been shot dead the minute he stepped across the frontier!

Blade went over to his own pallet and lay down on it. It looked as if this trip to Dimension X was going

110

to end in the same sort of confusion and frustration as it began. The only trouble was, he was probably going to end along with it.

It was time to get his own sleep, while the woman was between bouts of fever. It seemed to help her if he was sitting beside her. If he could do nothing else, he could try to see she didn't die alone. There were worse ways of spending his own last days.

Blade was awakened by the cell door crashing open. Four guards with drawn pistols tramped in. The pistols weren't lasers but heavy revolvers, with as much stopping power as a Home Dimension Magnum. They could disable a man even if they didn't hit him in a vital spot.

"Up!" snapped one guard. Blade rose swiftly. He wanted to appear frightened and submissive, to make the guards less alert.

Another guard bent over the dying woman and shook his head. "She won't last the day." He drew his revolver and shot the woman in the head. At least it was a more merciful death than being left alone in her last delirium.

The four guards made a square around Blade and marched into the corridor. Blade realized they were probably taking him somewhere else to experiment on him. Down the whitewashed corridor to an elevator, up what seemed like three or four floors, then out into another corridor. This one was brightly lit and hummed with activity behind closed doors of polished metal. It reminded Blade rather of the main corridor in the Project's Complex One.

At the end of the corridor a door led out onto a metal-railed balcony. Beyond the railing a cliff dropped off more than three hundred feet, to the plain where the missile station lay. Blade recognized the gantry, saw assembly buildings, radar stations, and warehouses, as well as humped shapes which might be blockhouses or fuel tanks. He also saw brightly polished construction robots at work on a number of what looked like missile silos.

In daylight, it was easy to see this wasn't just a research facility. It was also Doimar's main missile base. When the "Day" came, the germ warheads would be launched from those silos. And a fat lot of good this knowledge was likely to do Richard Blade!

The guards hustled Blade along the terrace toward the door at the far end. As they did, he thought he heard someone calling his name, so faint and far off he couldn't be sure he'd even heard anything aloud. Who would be calling him here? Nobody. He decided he was imagining things. Then as they reached the door the call came again.

This time Blade was sure he'd heard it, but not aloud. He'd heard it in his mind.

Who in this Dimension would be calling him mentally, even if they knew his name?

Cheeky?

Blade nearly said it out loud. Then he nearly said "Impossible," normally an obscene word in his vocabulary. Instead he thought his name as strongly as he could, while also holding a mental image of himself as he'd been in Home Dimension.

The reply came. It was a reply, no mistake about it. But it still might, just *might*, be a Doimari telepath.

Cheeky.

He thought the feather-monkey's name just as hard as his own, and projected Cheeky's image as clearly as he'd projected his own. Two of the guards looked at him suspiciously while the other two fumbled with the door.

Then suddenly pandemonium broke loose. An explosion roared above. Blade heard glass smash and saw smoke gush out of a window carved in the cliff two stories above the terrace. Then a small shape sailed out the window.

Even at a distance Blade recognized Cheeky. He held his breath as the feather-monkey slid a good way down the cliff. Even Cheeky might not be able

112

to find a firm grip, and it would be just too much to lose him now!

But Cheeky's fingers and toes were as sure as ever. He stopped his slide and began to crawl like a fly along the face of the cliff toward the terrace.

One of the guards followed Blade's eyes and saw Cheeky. He raised his pistol and sighted on the feather-monkey. To do this he had to turn his back on Blade. He seemed confident that the other three guards were enough to keep Blade out of trouble.

That was his last mistake. As his finger tightened on the trigger, Blade caught him by the hair with one hand and chopped him across the throat with the other. The guard died choking and Blade caught his pistol as it dropped from limp fingers. Blade put his back against the wall and covered the other three guards.

A moment later Cheeky reached the railing, balanced on it, then made a flying leap clear across the terrace onto Blade's shoulder. He was *yeeping* hysterically with joy and excitement. His thoughts were so jumbled that Blade didn't even try to follow them.

He also didn't try to understand how this miracle of Cheeky's return had come about. For now, it was enough that *Cheeky was back.*

Chapter 15

The three surviving guards weren't going to drop their guns, not with a comrade to avenge. On the other hand, they weren't quite crazy enough to draw as long as Blade had the drop on them.

They could go for their pistols the minute he blinked, though. How long could he keep from blinking?

Then a thought struck Blade. He filled his mind with a picture of Cheeky going around to the three guards and taking their pistols. He held the picture until he sensed that Cheeky was getting it, thinking it over, and beginning to calm down.

At last Cheeky gave a small *yeeep*, and threw his arms around Blade's head. For a moment Blade was afraid his vision would be blocked and the guards would take advantage of that fact. Then Cheeky jumped down from Blade's shoulder and trotted over to the first guard.

"Give him your pistol," said Blade. The guard stared at Blade, then at Cheeky, obviously wondering who was crazy. "You've got until I count four," said Blade. "One, two—"

At "three" the guard decided that obeying Blade was his only chance of staying alive until he could figure out what was happening. He dropped his pistol onto the terrace, and Cheeky picked it up. The other two guards did the same, and Cheeky returned

114

to Blade with one pistol in each hand and dragging the third with his tail.

For the moment, the immediate danger from the three guards was past. Blade suspected the next move was up to someone else.

Meanwhile, thick and greasy smoke kept pouring out the broken window. Blade wondered what Cheeky had done to escape. He got a reply in the form of a mental picture—Cheeky dashing around a laboratory, upsetting everything in sight until some chemicals finally spilled on a live wire. The feather-monkey also projected a picture of people in laboratory smocks running around screaming, their hair and clothing on fire. He seemed rather happy about their fate.

For the first time Blade noticed that Cheeky was so gaunt his ribs were showing. Some of his feathers had been singed off, and bare skin showed where others had been deliberately plucked out. He'd been treated as an experimental animal, and not too well-treated at that! If so, then it seemed to Blade that the Doimari Seekers were getting just about what they deserved.

The guards became more nervous as the uproar from the laboratory grew. They looked about ready to jump Blade, when suddenly the door flew open. A man in a smoke-grimed laboratory coat ran out, followed by a young woman. The man took one look at Cheeky on Blade's shoulder, then cursed.

"What are you doing with that little monster?" he snarled. "Give him back or—"

Blade showed the scientist the muzzle of his pistol. "First, you tell me where you found him and what you've been—"

"Who are you to ask *me*?" the scientist blustered, ignoring the pistol.

"Erhon, don't be foolish," said the woman. "Blue Boy might have been that man's pet. He could tell—"

The scientist ignored his assistant just as thoroughly as he had ignored the pistol, and he plunged a hand into his pocket. Blade couldn't wait to find what

115

might be in there. He put a bullet into the scientist's chest, then another as the man seemed slow to go down. The second shot slammed him up against the railing. He slid down into a sitting position as his coat turned red. A small laser fell out of his pocket as he rolled over on his side.

Blade picked up a second pistol, since there was no way to reload the one he had. The young woman was staring wildly at everything without focusing on anything.

"I'm sorry I had to shoot him," said Blade quietly. "But he shouldn't have tried to draw on me. Now, will you calm down and go tell whoever's in charge here that I want to talk to him? Blue Boy *was* mine. I lost him a long time ago, and thought I'd never find him again. If you'll let both of us go free, you may learn something useful." The girl hesitated, her mouth quivering. "Go on," said Blade sharply. "You can have hysterics later!"

The girl ran back into the laboratory complex without closing the door behind her. Blade settled down to wait. He hoped she would get word to somebody sensible before somebody stupid decided to snipe Blade with a laser rifle. He shifted so that he could cover the guards and look around at the same time, but knew that precaution wouldn't help much. A laser rifle or even a gunpowder one would far outrange his pistols.

Instead of a laser's whipcrack, the next thing Blade heard was the whine of a lifter's propellers. Then a shadow passed overhead, and a disembodied voice boomed over the terrace.

"Commander Voros! You asked for whoever's in charge, I am he. Put down your pistols, and I give you my word of honor as a Seeker that no harm will come to you."

"Tell those guards to move to the end of the terrace first," shouted Blade. "I don't trust them." He didn't trust the voice coming from the lifters either, but there was nothing he could do about that. And Blue Boy doesn't get hurt, either." Cheeky *yeeeped* in agreement.

"All right. Move, you idiots!"

The guards jumped at the voice as if Blade had finally shot them. Then they scurried to the far end of the terrace, as the small lifter swept in. A laser jutted from its nose, and a pilot and a passenger sat in the cockpit. Ten feet above the terrace the passenger opened the door, and five feet up he jumped out without waiting for the machine to land.

He came down on his feet with catlike grace, not even going to his knees. He'd called himself a Seeker but to Blade he looked more like a rather sinister sort of soldier. He wore a black coverall, black boots, and a close-fitting black helmet. The only color on him anywhere was the dark red plastic butt of a heavy laser pistol in a black leather shoulder holster. His hair and eyes were also black.

He stepped up to Blade. He was about the same height but slimmer. "I am Detcharn, First Seeker and *Du-Shro* of Doimar." That meant he was not only chief of scientific research but something like chief of staff of the armed forces. *A man in charge indeed,* thought Blade.

"I am honored," he said.

"That remains to be seen," replied Detcharn. "Tell me your story."

Blade did so, emphasizing the bond between him and Cheeky/Blue Boy and how all efforts to learn anything about the feather-monkey would now be useless without his cooperation. He did not try to find out how Cheeky had wound up in Doimar. He badly wanted to know, but there would be better times to ask . . . if he lived long enough!

When Blade was finished, Detcharn raised his bushy black eyebrows. "What makes you think we want to learn anything about this little beast worth letting you go free?"

"Don't try bluffing me, Detcharn. You know he's a

telepath. Otherwise why would you have spent all this time and effort studying him?" Blade remembered how the scientist's assistant had started to say that Blade could tell them something. What it was exactly they needed to know was unclear, but Blade decided against quoting the girl. She would be in enough trouble without her slip being passed on to Detcharn, who did not look like a forgiving man.

"Indeed, you may be right. To be sure, we might need a telepath to examine *you*."

Blade didn't hesitate. "Then get one. I don't have anywhere to go for a while, and neither do you."

"It's hardly tactful to hold me hostage," said Detcharn. Then he smiled, which gave him a sort of wolfish charm. "But in your position I wouldn't be tactful either. Very well." He spoke briefly into a small radio on his wrist, and the lifter darted away.

Again Blade settled down to wait. It was a gamble, that a Doimari telepath could prove the link between him and Cheeky without revealing his identity. But he hardly had anything to lose. The alternative was tamely accepting certain and probably unpleasant death; this way he could at least hope to take one of Doimar's most valuable leaders with him.

The telepath couldn't have been far away. The lifter was back in less than twenty minutes, although they were a long twenty minutes for Blade. The guards were too far away to be dangerous, even if they'd wanted to defy their leader. Detcharn himself was another matter. From the way he moved, Blade knew he was in perfect condition and might be an unarmed-combat expert.

This time the lifter landed on the terrace. The new passenger was a slim brown-haired woman, with enormous gray eyes in a pale face, dressed in a long flowing blue gown. There was something virginal and even slightly otherworldly about her.

"Read him," ordered Detcharn. The lifter took off, and the blast from its propeller made the wom-

118

an's hair fly out behind her like a flag. She patted it into position, came up to Blade, put one hand on his chest and another on his forehead, and screwed her own face up into a look of total concentration.

Blade had just time to form a mental picture of himself and Cheeky in Kaldak and hold it. He didn't have time to make a convincing picture of him and the feather-monkey doing anything. It was a static image, and he was more than slightly worried that the telepathic woman would be able to detect the image for what it was—an effort to deceive her and block her from learning the truth.

Blade suppressed the worry vigorously. *Any* unusual emotion might give the woman a clue. Cheeky was at least that sensitive to Blade's emotions; why shouldn't a human telepath be even more so?

At least he wouldn't have to warn Cheeky not to cooperate with anyone in Doimar. After the treatment he'd received and the vengeance he'd taken, Cheeky would let himself be plucked naked rather than help the Doimari or betray the friend he'd found again after so long.

The mental pulses Blade felt were so faint and fumbling that at times he wasn't sure if they were there at all. They lasted for quite a while, though, and he saw sweat on the woman's forehead. He hoped she wouldn't collapse. Detcharn would simply bring in another telepath, who might be more powerful or at least forewarned. He also might try other, more physical methods of interrogation.

At last the woman started to vibrate all over like a plucked harpstring. She closed her eyes and stepped away from Blade, then caught at the railing with both hands. Blade gripped her shoulders to make sure she didn't lose balance and fall. She twisted out of his grasp, went to her knees, and vomited.

At last she rose, wiped her mouth with the sleeve of her robe, and turned back to Detcharn. "He is telling the truth about himself and the—he calls it Cheeky. To Voros, Cheeky is not an animal. And they do speak mind to mind, in a way I have never met before."

"A way worth studying?"

"Certainly, if any form of mind-to-mind speech is worth studying. I thought we had decided that long ago." She met Detcharn's sharp look fearlessly. "Also, we will study it much better when Cheeky recovers from what he has suffered in there." If her eyes had been lasers, the look she threw at the laboratory door would have melted it.

Detcharn shrugged. "Well, Eshorn has paid already." The telepath shuddered and Cheeky *yeeeped* as they both seemed to pick up ugly thoughts from Detcharn. "As for these fools ..." He turned toward the three guards, drew his laser, and shot one in the belly. The other two stood as if paralyzed until their comrade started to scream.

One of them backed away, as if he wanted to melt into the cliff and get away. The other charged Detcharn. The black-clad man put his laser down and waited for the guard in unarmed-combat stance. His face showed something horribly like lust. Blade found his own hands itching to pick up Detcharn and pitch him over the balcony.

It wasn't a fight, any more than it's a fight when a cat kills a mouse. Detcharn toyed with the man for a couple of minutes, even letting him land one or two harmless blows. Then swiftly he broke the man's left arm, chopping him across the throat, and levered him over the railing. The man screamed all the way down the cliff to his landing in a puff of dust.

The last guard didn't wait to find out what Detcharn had in mind for him. He went over the railing by himself, and fell silently down the three hundred feet to the plain.

Detcharn wiped his hands on the clothing of the still-living first guard. Blade, the telepath, and Cheeky watched in silence. Cheeky's tail was curled tightly under his body. Blade scratched his head to relax

120

the feather-monkey, although he himself felt anything but relaxed.

The telepath went over to the dying guard and laid her hands on his forehead. After a moment his eyes closed and he stopped moaning. Had she simply blocked the pain, or actually willed him to death?

"Even for you, Detcharn, was this not more than what was needed?" asked the telepath. Her face was a mask and her voice toneless.

Detcharn started. "No! Never! Such will always be needed, with fools who stand between me and what I must do! Has your wish to cleanse our blood and avenge the great defeat weakened so much? If it has, *you* should fear me, Moshra."

"I am past fearing you, Detcharn," said Moshra. "And my desire to prove the worth of our blood is as strong as yours. Does that mean I can have no opinion of my own, as to the best *way* of proving it? If you think so, you are the only man in Doimar who does?"

After a moment, Detcharn shrugged. "Very well, sister. I will be less quick with the guards and other weapons-bearers. I cannot guard my back against all of them, and with the Day so close . . ." His fingers writhed like snakes. "Then everyone will know that the blood of the Sky Master Blade has finally given the victory to Doimar."

Blade looked quickly from one face to another. There was a family resemblance. And now that he looked more closely, both of them had something else in common. . . .

"The Sky Master Blade?" Blade chose his words and controlled his voice carefully. He also hoped Moshra could only read his mind while touching him!

"Yes. He was father to both of us," snapped Detcharn. "Us and four others. The Kaldakans think they got the best from Blade, because he betrayed us. But they will learn otherwise, when a son of their precious Sky Master brings them down. Oh, yes, they will learn, and soon." The lustful look was back on his face. Moshra turned away and looked firmly out over the plain.

After a moment, Blade joined her. This Dimension seemed to be producing weird family reunions! First Baliza with her attempted seduction, and now Moshra with her telepathy and Detcharn with his mad drive to prove that her father's blood did not taint him.

Blade gripped the railing hard, until his knuckles turned white. The urge to kill Detcharn was back again, even stronger than before. So was sheer nausea, that this homicidal maniac—there was no other word for it—was his son.

My son, thought Blade. *What have I unleashed on this Dimension, by playing stud with the women of Doimar the first time I was here?*

And another thought: *What can I do to get it back on the leash?*

Stating the problem he had to solve calmed him and got his mind working again. The next time Detcharn spoke to him, Blade was even able to reply normally. At least Detcharn didn't notice anything wrong, and Moshra still stood with her back to the two men.

Chapter 16

Blade quickly realized the missile base was the key to defeating Detcharn's plans and ending any immediate threat to Kaldak. Detcharn was so proud of the missiles that he hadn't bothered to develop any other way of spreading the fever germs. If the missile silos were wrecked and Kaldak warned of what they might be facing, there would be no quick war ending in an easy victory for Doimar. Blade could hope that Detcharn wouldn't persuade the Doimari to follow him in a long war. He seemed the type to make enemies who would take advantage of his first defeat to get rid of him for good.

Blade wished he could be sure of this, but quickly learned he wasn't going to know this or a lot of other things about the new Doimar. He was no longer a prisoner, but he was still something less than a guest. He was seldom allowed outside the research complex, and neither the guards nor the Seekers would answer his questions.

Detcharn talked freely, but Blade didn't learn much from him. Most of what Detcharn said was boasting about his past achievements or his future plans. He seemed to have vague notions about ruling not only Doimar but the whole Dimension as a dictator, after the fall of Kaldak. It didn't seem to bother him that he might be ruling over an empire of corpses.

Once he disappeared for several days, then came back to invite Blade to a private showing of some films. They showed a raid on a Tribal village. Blade watched with disgust at the ruthless butchery, and also with interest at the close-ups of the Tribesmen. Many of them had the long, hairy, pointed ears of the young chief he'd let escape from the Doimari tracking station. Was this the same Tribe, or was the mutation just a coincidence?

Detcharn was so proud of the raid and the number of Tribesmen he'd killed personally that Blade was able to draw him out. "I hate to sound like Moshra, but was the raid necessary? You got off lightly this time, but what if they're waiting for you the next time?"

Detcharn shrugged. "Our soldiers know getting killed is part of their job. But I'm not planning another such raid any time soon. Perhaps not at all, if the Day comes soon enough. This was the Tribe that ran off from our ranging and tracking station and let it fall to Kaldak. They had to be punished."

So this Tribe might indeed be the young chief's. Interesting—and maybe useful, since they now had no cause to love Doimar. If Detcharn just hadn't killed off so many of their warriors that they might now be helpless . . .

"Killing them won't bring back your old station," said Blade reprovingly. "It might even provoke other Tribes to attack your new one, whenever you set it up."

"Oh, it's been in operation for some time now," said Detcharn. "I will send you out there to see it yourself in a few days. And you're right, we should patrol the area around it more closely. But the Tribes spend too much time fighting each other to ever unite against us *or* Kaldak. Also, the new station is a good hundred miles from the nearest Tribe with Newtec weapons. Long before they can find it and send warriors that far, the Day will fall on them as it will on Kaldak." He dismissed adding the Tribesmen to his planned genocide with an airy wave of his hand and poured more drinks.

124

At least Blade needed no help to learn about the missile base. It was all laid out in front of him anytime he stepped out on the terrace, which he did about twice a day. He quickly memorized every key point so thoroughly he could have easily built a model of the base.

Taking out the base was not going to be a one-man job. Blade knew that almost at once. But twenty or thirty men armed to the teeth and taking it by surprise would have a chance. Forty or fifty would have a very good one. There were usually less than a hundred guards, they were scattered widely, and only a few of the Seekers bothered to carry weapons. The base was also a couple of hours' flying time from Doimar itself. The raiders could do their work and be long gone before reinforcements arrived.

Assuming you could conjure up the men needed, how likely was surprise? There Blade had to do more guessing than he liked, but finally decided that the chances were good enough to make the raid worth trying if he could get the men. The Doimari seemed to assume that the Kaldakans not only didn't know about the base but couldn't have done anything if they knew. There were virtually no antiaircraft defenses and all the radar sets were used for tracking missiles as they took off.

And if all else failed, there was still a one-man job which could upset Doimar's plans. Blade could kill Detcharn.

Killing his own son wasn't something Blade would normally have been contemplating this calmly. But then, normally he wouldn't have had to contemplate it at all. It was a tragedy that a mind as brilliant as Detcharn's had to be destroyed, but that very brilliance meant there was no one to take his place.

Of course Blade's own chances of survival afterward would be small. But he'd made up his mind on that point, too. Detcharn was too dangerous to be allowed to live.

*   *   *

"More wine, Voros?"

"Thank you, Moshra." Blade held his cup out as she poured from a crystal jug. It was good wine, tart and strong.

Through the picture window he saw the distant glow of the research base on the horizon. This was the second time Moshra had invited him to dinner. It was the first time she'd brought him to her private villa several miles from the base. Blade wondered if he was facing a second attempt by one of his daughters to seduce him.

Conversation died as they drank. The glow on the horizon brightened momentarily. After a bit the house started vibrating and gently. The rumble of the launch swelled, then died away.

"They're sending one off almost every night," said Moshra. Her voice was so toneless it was impossible to tell if she approved or not. Blade studied her as a woman, setting aside for the moment their blood relationship.

She was actually quite attractive, or would have been if she hadn't been wearing a shapeless gown and pulled her thick brown hair back into a tight knot. She also had the same remote, impersonal manner as when he'd first met her. He wondered if telepaths were required to be celibate?

Instead he said, "Your mind seems to be far away tonight. I might be in Kaldak for all the attention your're paying me."

She blushed, then managed a smile. "My mind has to be some distance away from yours. Otherwise it might be *in* yours."

"You don't have to touch me?"

"I can reach you more strongly when I am touching you. But even without that, I might read thoughts you did not want known." She sighed. "Being able to speak mind to mind is a great gift—they say. I have not always been better off for having it, though. But I think a good time is coming." She reached out and held Blade's hand.

126

Blade suppressed a start, then the urge to pull away. The gesture was so clumsy that he could hardly believe it had any sexual meaning. Or did Moshra want to get rid of her virginity, if she had it, but didn't quite know how to go about persuading him to help her?

That was as far as he let his guessing go before he clamped a barrier over his mind. Cheeky *yeeeped* in protest. Blade tossed him a piece of bread with his free hand but didn't relax his mental control. He couldn't jerk his hand away without causing a scene, and as long as Moshra was touching him she could far too easily detect the questions he was asking in his mind.

Moshra's free hand fluttered over the wine jug like a moth around a candle flame. Suddenly it jerked convulsively, and the jug toppled off the table. Wine and shards of crystal made a mess on the rug.

"Oh, curse the—" began Moshra, but Blade was no longer listening to her. He'd heard a sound where no sound should be, from the curtained alcove in the rear of the room. His chair went over with a thump as he jumped up, and he was drawing his pistol as he whirled around.

Then the curtains parted and revealed a heavy-set, white-haired woman in a powered wheelchair. She pressed a button and the wheelchair rolled out into the room. Then her face split in a familiar grin.

"Welcome back to Doimar, Richard Blade."

Chapter 17

It was Feragga, the woman who had ruled Doimar when Blade last visited.

Blade had heard of people's hearts stopping from sheer surprise. He came closer to having the experience than he liked this time. However, his mind kept working. He even kept some control over his mouth.

"I suppose there'd be no point in suggesting that you're imagining things in thinking I'm Richard Blade?" he asked drily.

"Of course not," said Feragga with her old bluntness. "After Moshra's reading of your thoughts, I don't care a pile of munfan dung who you say you are. I know you're Blade." She rolled her wheelchair close to the table. "Pour me a drink, Moshra."

"Mother Feragga, do you think you should?"

"I don't think about what I should or shouldn't do, Moshra. I haven't the time left to waste on thinking about such things. I just go on the way I did, and that means wine when I want it. Or do you want your father to pour it?"

Blade grinned. Feragga hadn't changed a bit. She was still accustomed to getting what she wanted, when she wanted it. Moshra sighed and poured the wine. Feragga drank thirstily, smacking her lips.

"Good. Thank whoever's done it that I can still taste. When that goes, I *will* be ready for laying out and burning." She set the cup back on the table and stared at Blade. "You haven't aged hardly at all. I suppose time passes at a different rate, where you spent the last thirty years?"

"It obviously does," said Blade. If Feragga and Moshra had dug out his major secret, there wasn't much point arguing over the minor ones. There also wasn't much point in wasting time with polite conversation. Feragga couldn't have brought him here just to talk about old times.

"You're still a canny soul, aren't you?" said Feragga. "Well, I hardly expected anything else, and indeed it makes me glad. You'll understand what I want of you, and you'll do it better."

"Mother Feragga—" began Moshra again, but a shake of the white head silenced her.

"Remember how much trouble it took to get me out here tonight without anyone konwing?" Feragga said. "And remember that every new trip means more danger of discovery. Then think—do we have that much time to spare?"

"No."

"I knew you'd see it my way." She turned back to Blade. "First, let me just tell you that I adopted your daughter, Moshra, after her natural mother died in childbirth. In this way, I was able to have one of your children for my own, even though my seed was dry when you visited here last. I had great plans for Moshra and Doimar, but then Detcharn began assuming more and more power. I was considered too feeble to be a threat, so I was left alone, but that's where Detcharn made his greatest mistake. Blade, I want you to escape from Doimar and warn Kaldak of what Detcharn plans."

Blade wasn't an easy man to surprise, and he'd already had one surprise this evening big enough to make everything else look puny. So he merely shrugged. "Easier said than done. And what if I think it's a trap?"

Moshra winced, but Feragga only laughed. "If you hadn't asked that question, I might have doubted

129

you were the same Blade. I'll speak plainly. You do what I tell you, or *I* tell Detcharn who you are."

"If you want to attack him, should you give him that kind of knowledge?"

"I've give him the blood out of my heart if it would take his attention off his plans!" snarled Feragga. "Trying to find out how you came back from wherever you were will do that. Also, the Kaldakans will learn your secret sooner or later. Then they'll stop at nothing to get you back. Detcharn and the Seekers will be busy trying to prevent them. More attention gone elsewhere. It could go on like that for years. Meanwhile, sooner or later I can find someone else to get the secret to Kaldak. Not as good as you, maybe, but good enough for the job."

So if he didn't cooperate, he would be thrown to the wolves, and the Dimension X secret would be up the bloody spout! "You haven't changed either, Feragga."

"Thank you. I've tried not to, at least until there is peace between Doimar and Kaldak. There can't be until Detcharn's scheme is defeated."

She lowered her voice. "I do not love Kaldak, Blade. I do not even love you that much. But I do not love at all the idea of Detcharn ruling over a land of corpses and ruins, which is what he will do if he is not stopped."

Blade said nothing. If he and Feragga agreed that much, he didn't need to. It was still ironic, that this time he would be escaping from Doimar to warn Kaldak with her blessing instead of her curse. He made a business of pouring himself some more wine, while he considered her proposal for possible traps. He didn't entirely trust her, and he wasn't going to trust at all to luck if he could help it. Not with so much at stake.

"I'll do it," he said finally. "But one condition. I take the formula for the fever vaccine with me. That way Kaldak will be protected even if nothing else happens to Detcharn and the Seekers."

130

Feragga's bushy eyebrows rose. "Why should I do that?"

"So I can be sure that *no one* in Doimar can ever use the fever against Kaldak."

A long silence. "You don't trust me," said Feragga at last.

"Not enough to leave *everything* in your hands," said Blade. "I learned that early, in a hard school. Come on, Feragga. It won't do you any good if I tell Detcharn about this conversation, will it?" He saw her swallow and knew he was right.

However, she wasn't going to give up without a fight. "What good would that do you, Blade? Your secret would be out anyway, and Detcharn isn't given to gratitude. You'd have as much to fear from him as ever."

"Not if he thought he had to conduct a purge of your friends before he could move. That would also keep him busy."

"You would be signing Moshra's death warrant as well as mine, Blade. Do you care so little for your daughter?"

Before Blade had to pretend that he didn't, Moshra slammed her hand down on the table angrily. "Mother Feragga, enough of this! If you go on asking for what my father will not give, we will get nothing. I am certain he would see us both die rather than do less than what he thinks is his duty. So if you will not talk sense, I will give him the formula myself."

"How did *you* come to know it?" said Feragga, startled.

Moshra blushed and bowed her head. "I could not help learning it from Detcharn's mind once when—when I was lying with him?"

"Your own brother?" said Blade.

"Half-brother," she corrected him in a flat voice. "He—he is proud of being bound by no Law—except—his own will. He—Father, why are you looking like that?"

Feragga gave a bawdy chuckle. "I'll wager his

131

daughter Baliza tried to bed him in Kaldak. There's a lusty wench, by all reports. She wouldn't have known who he was, of course. Just seen a fine piece of man's flesh and wanted to grab."

"Mother Feragga, do you read thoughts, too?"

"No, I just know more about the ways of men and women than you do." She sighed. "Blade, since it's doing things your way or not at all—so be it."

Over the last of the wine they worked out the details. Blade would make his planned trip to the new tracking station. Moshra would go with him. So would a soldier in Feragga's pay. Halfway to the station, the soldier would "hijack" the lifter by killing the pilot. Then Blade would take over.

"You can handle one of our lifters, I hope?" Feragga asked Blade.

"Well enough to get it and us down in one piece."

"Good."

Blade would then fly the lifter to a place free of Tribesmen, near the border with Kaldak. They would abandon the lifter and destroy it, then march overland into Kaldakan territory. After that it would be up to Blade. He would still need some luck, but with the serum formula to bargain with he thought he could manage.

"Make sure you destroy the lifter so thoroughly that no one will suspect it wasn't an accident," Feragga insisted.

"Why?" said Blade. He thought he knew, but wanted to draw her out anyway.

"It will be my neck otherwise," she said. "And while it's an old stiff neck, I'd like to keep it in one piece a little longer if I can. Also, I don't want civil war in Doimar."

She explained. The regular army of Doimar hadn't really forgiven the Seekers for their retreat in the great battle against Kaldak. Only Feragga herself had kept them from destroying the Seekers after the battle. Now only Detcharn kept the two factions working together. He was as good a soldier as he was a scientist, even though he had become a brutal tyrant, obsessed with the destruction of Kaldak.

"If it is learned, however, that the lifter was sent in order to warn Kaldak of Detcharn's plans, the soldiers will probably rise up against the Seekers. The Seekers will fight back. Neither side will win, but there will be many dead, and Doimar will not recover. I want peace not only between the soldiers and Seekers, but also between two strong cities. I do not want the Doimari to be slaves of Kaldak."

"I wouldn't ask it," said Blade. Also, the Seekers of Doimar were still the best and most advanced scientists in this Dimension. If they survived until peace broke out between the two big cities, the whole Dimension would benefit.

He still wasn't entirely happy with the thought of leaving Detcharn alive. No victory would be complete and no peace secure without his death. Even if his scheme for germ warfare was defeated, he might have a few other cards up his sleeve. What about hydrogen bombs, with the fusion reaction started by lasers instead of by a nuclear explosion?

However, this made it even more important to keep Blade's escape a secret. As long as Detcharn didn't know his plans were exposed, he would not use some other weapon against which Kaldak might have no defenses.

Blade would be buying time, no more. But if he bought enough, perhaps he could safely leave to others the job of killing Detcharn.

Chapter 18

The lifter whined through the night sky. The interior was dark, except for the lights on the instrument panel. Blade could barely make out Moshra's face beside him. The soldier squatting aft by the open door was only a dim shape.

"*Yeeep?*" It was a question from Cheeky. He'd learned to communicate with Blade mostly by sound when Moshra was around. He didn't entirely trust her even if Blade thought he should. He definitely didn't like his thoughts being overheard by anyone except Blade or another Feathered One. This made communication between him and Blade a little slow and vague when Moshra was around.

"Not long now," said Blade. "We must be at least halfway." The pilot overheard him and nodded. "More like two-thirds," he said. "But this is the difficult-part. We're over Tribal lands, and the Tribes don't like us much anymore, since . . ." He let his voice trail off. The regular armed forces of Doimar had been proud of winning the friendship of the Tribes, and didn't approve of Detcharn's bloodthirsty raid. However, they also couldn't speak out against Detcharn as long as he was Doimar's chief hope of victory.

"The Kaldakans have helped us, then," said Blade. "They took out a lot of the Newtec weapons the Tribes had, while I was in Kaldak. I doubt if they have anything which can hit you up here."

"I hope not," said the pilot. He made a minute adjustment of the controls. The lifter tilted slightly and swung onto a new course.

The soldier hadn't said anything during this exchange. But then, he hadn't spoken five words since the lifter took off. Blade wondered if the man was just naturally close-mouthed, or whether he was getting nervous. A nervous man would be a bad choice for this little job. Of course he'd been handpicked by Feragga, but Feragga wasn't a professional at intelligence work; and Blade didn't really trust anyone who wasn't—

Come on, Richard, he told himself. *You're starting to jump at shadows. That's no way to go, even with this much at stake.*

The trouble was, he couldn't quite forget how much *was* at stake.

Slowly, to keep both the soldier and the pilot from noticing it, Blade shifted his seat. Now he was no longer in the direct line of fire between the soldier and the pilot. He also unbuttoned the flap of his holster.

Suddenly the soldier let out a wild scream. The pilot jumped and turned in his seat, just in time to receive a laser blast in the face. His face became a ghastly charred mask but somehow he didn't die. Blade started to rise but Moshra was on her feet first. He reached for her hand, to pull her down.

"No. I've sworn an oath to use my mind-speaking for help at times like this." She jerked free and stepped toward the dying pilot. This brought her directly into the path of the soldier. Like a striking snake, one arm of the soldier looped around her throat, while the other hand rammed his pistol into her back. She started to struggle, then stopped at his growl.

"You be still, or I shoot your friend. Same goes the other way, too." He pointed the gun at Blade. "Now you go and take the controls. Then fly us where I tell you?"

135

"To Detcharn?"

The arm tightened around Moshra's neck. "Just fly. Don't talk."

Blade decided this was the wrong time to try anything to subdue the disloyal soldier. He'd wait and find his opportunity when Moshra would have a better chance. Keeping his hands in clear view, he put his pistol on the seat. Then he started toward the empty copilot's seat.

"Soldier," said Moshra. "If Feragga isn't paying you enough—ehhhkkkk!" as the arm tightened around her throat.

"She can't pay enough to bring back my father. The damned Kaldakans killed him. She can't keep Detcharn's hands off my wife and baby, either."

"If it's Detcharn worrying you—" began Blade, but the soldier's reply was snarled.

"Fly, curse you, or she dies slow. Guts burned out, breasts burned off. Fly!"

Blade turned back to the controls. They were a standard set. With a little practice he knew he could tilt the lifter sharply. That would throw the soldier off-balance. No tricks now, though. The soldier sounded taut-nerved and much too ready to kill.

Moshra must have thought the same thing, but felt she had less to lose. The soldier backed toward the rear of the cabin, still gripping her tightly. As they came opposite the open door, Moshra went limp. At the same time she rammed her elbows wildly backward.

By pure luck one elbow caught the soldier in his groin. He howled and fired. His aim was wild, and he only hit the control panel. He fired again, and the beam scorched Blade's cheek.

Then Moshra's full weight came on the soldier. He lurched backward, lost his balance, and went out the door. Unfortunately he clutched Moshra's gown as he went, and dragged her with him.

Blade knew he wouldn't forget his daughter's scream as she fell, not if he lived to be a thousand years old.

136

He got to the door just as Moshra and the soldier vanished into the darkness below. He clung numbly to the door frame, until he heard Cheeky's cries and felt the lifter starting to wander all over the sky. Then he clamped an iron lid on what he felt and turned back to business.

The pilot was mercifully dead, and both sets of controls hopelessly wrecked. The pilot's parachute was also too badly burned to be used safely. Fortunately the copilot's chute was intact in its rack under the seat. Blade pulled it out and buckled it on. Then he took all the spare rope he could find in the cabin and tied Cheeky to the harness across his chest. The feather-monkey wasn't going to be comfortable, but he'd be safe, and Blade would have both hands free to control his parachute lines.

Cheeky made no protest. He sensed that the woman Moshra whom he'd never liked had meant something to his master and friend. He did not want to anger his master when he felt grief and loss. Also, he sensed even more strongly that there was danger coming, and his master was trying to save both of them from it. He wouldn't do anything to interfere with that, either. He'd lost Blade once, then found him again in a way he still didn't understand. He would go through almost anything rather than lose Blade again.

When Cheeky was securely tied in place, Blade pried open the floor plate which gave access to the main power cable to the lift-field generator. With a quick blast of his laser, he fused the cable. The generator died with a rumble and a screech, and the lifter nosed down for its final dive. As it did, Blade clutched the ripcord of his parachute and hurled himself through the door.

There was enough wind at ground level to take Blade on a merry ride as his chute dragged him across the ground. He finally spilled the air from it just as he reached the edge of a ravine and slid down

137

it into a marsh. He got out of it as fast as he'd got in, but not fast enough to keep himself and Cheeky dry. Both of them were soaked to the skin in filthy, stinking water.

Cheeky ran around, jumping up and down to dry himself and raking the slimy mud out of his feathers with his paws. Blade sent him a mental message to be quiet, but otherwise ignored him.

Blade wanted to laugh, because he knew he might weep if he didn't laugh. Except that if he started laughing he might not be able to stop. . . . Finally he squatted on the ground and considered what to do next.

This return to Kaldak was breaking all records for danger and confusion. Things were likely to get worse before they got better, too, if they ever *did* get better. He didn't dare think about Moshra's death, but apart from that, he was stranded in probably hostile territory, a long way from the Kaldakan border. He wasn't even completely sure how to get there! If he took too long, Detcharn's "Day" might come before he could warn Kaldak. If he ran hostile Tribesmen, he and his warning might never reach Kaldak at all.

Things could be worse, however. He had the serum formula on him. The lifter's wreck would probably look like a normal crash. Finally, the soldier seemed to have been acting on his own, hoping for Detcharn's reward. There was a reasonable chance that Detcharn did not know and would not learn of Feragga's scheme until it was too late.

He'd have to move fast, though. That meant no searching for Moshra's body. She would have to lie out in the wind and the rain. His daughter would be a prey to scavengers until she rotted. His daughter—

A spasm of dreadful rage knotted Blade's stomach, and he vomited himself empty. When he'd wiped his mouth, he stood up and called Cheeky to him. The feather-monkey jumped up onto Blade's shoulder in silence. He sensed even more strongly than before that his master was not at peace with the world.

As he set off, it occurred to Blade that he had one more card to play if he had to. If he found a Tribe who didn't shoot first and ask questions afterward, he could claim to be an enemy of Doimar. That might win him a safe-conduct through their lands, although he doubted if they would take him all the way to Kaldak. New enemies didn't always wipe out the memory of old wars.

And he'd certainly be telling the truth! He was an enemy of Doimar—above all, of one particular Doimari. If he'd known that he was going to die the next minute, Blade would have gone gladly if he could have spent his last moments killing his monstrous son.

Indeed, that goal might even be achieved if Blade could persuade, if not the Kaldakans then at least the Tribes, that they must take action against their enemy. Someone—anyone—had to see to it that every last rocket of Detcharn—and Detcharn himself—was destroyed.

Chapter 19

Shangbari was the best hunter of the Red Cat Tribe. Others beside himself said this was so, and the sacred four-legged Red Cats gave no signs against it. So he was willing to believe it.

This meant he had to appear invincible in battle, always successful in finding game for the cooking fires of the Tribe, and afraid of nothing at all. Most of the time he succeeded, and he was able to hide the times he did not. Also, after the Doimar sky-killers came recently and slew so many of the Red Cats, Ikhnan the Chief forbade challenges and duels among the warriors.

"We have hardly the strength to keep the Red Cats from becoming a dead Tribe, like the Salamanders, the Grass Eaters, and the Tree Folk," Ikhnan said. "We have none to waste in fighting battles over small things."

"My reputation is not a small thing," Shangbari replied.

"It certainly will be very small, if you fight any duels over it," said Ikhnan. "I will see to that."

Shangbari took the threat seriously. Although Ikhran was no more than twenty-one hunting seasons old, he was wise as a Grandfather and fearless as a Death Pig. What he promised, he would do, or die trying—and if Shangbari caused Ikhnan's death, he would not live to gain anything by it. The very women and children of the Tribe would tear his flesh

140

from his bones and feed it to the sacred Red Cats, if the beasts did not turn up their black noses at it.

It did not help either that the Kaldakans and the Doimari between them had slain or driven away much of the game. Shangbari still brought back more than any other hunter, but not as much as before. Often it was not enough to feed all the hungry mouths in the villages of the Red Cats.

However, it was neither his reputation nor Ikhran's nor the shortage of game making Shangbari uneasy today. As he walked softly under a sullen gray sky, his rifle held ready, he would have given much to know what kind of man he was tracking. Not knowing this was what made him uneasy.

Once he'd seen a footprint, where the man had stepped on soft ground without knowing it. The footprint showed a City boot, whether of Kaldak or of Doimar Shangbari could not tell. That should mean a City man, for the Tribes had never taken to City clothing as they had to City weapons.

Yet he'd seen only that one footprint. No City man had ever left so few traces of his passage. Only a hunter of the Tribes could do that. In fact, Shangbari wondered if the man had left the footprint deliberately, as a sign for those tracking him. Did he want to be found? Was he mad? Or was he playing with Shangbari like a Red Cat with a mouse?

Shangbari drove that last thought from his mind. Soberly, he had to admit that he was closer to losing the trail than he'd ever been with a human quarry. Death Pigs were shrewder than a man in covering their trails, although if tracked down they could be trusted to charge headlong. It was a good thing that Death Pigs had no hands to hold rifles or even spears. Otherwise they would rule the land, not men.

Shangbari stopped at the edge of a field of long grass sloping down to a little stream. He raised his head and sniffed the air, then spread his ears as wide as he could. Any scent, any sound from his opponent would be more than he'd had for some time. As he sniffed and listened, he watched the field and the trees bordering it on three sides. He did not expect to see anything, but perhaps he could discover some of the places where the man had *not* gone. He felt foolish at hoping for so little, he, Shangbari, hunter of the Red Cats, but—

He heard the sound, and a heartbeat later knew that it was *behind* him. He had no chance to do anything with this knowledge. A knee crashed into the small of Shangbari's back. A leg scythed his feet out from under him. And an arm like the branch of a great tree went around his throat, choking off his breath. Something went *yeeeeep!* shrilly in his ear.

He did have one last thought before he heard nothing more: had he been tracking a wizard, who could send his body from one place to another without touching the ground? Or had he even been tracking something which was not a man at all?

When Shangbari's senses returned, he was lying on his back in the grass, bound hand and foot. The bonds were snug but not painful, as if his captor wished him helpless but not uncomfortable.

At least it was good to think that. A wizard would not have needed ropes to tie a captive. A nonhuman or a hostile Tribesman would have probably killed him outright. So his captor might be none of these things.

Or at least he could hope so.

Shangbari studied his captor. He was certainly a City man, from the way he dressed, but he was paler-skinned than anyone Shangbari had ever seen. He was also half a head taller than the hunter, with muscles in proportion. Certainly he'd have needed no wizardry to bring Shangbari down. He had a Doimari Oltec rifle across his knees, and he was munching on a piece of Newtec food from a pack beside him.

Shangbari's rifle also lay beside him, apparently undamaged. Then Shangbari saw who or *what* was sitting by the rifle, which started him thinking about wizardry again.

The creature was shaped like a man, except for its tail, but it was only about two feet high. Also, though it had no sign of wings, it was covered with feathers like a bird. The City man might be human, but surely his companion was not. Might the companion be the wizard, and the City man his servant? That frightened Shangbari all over again.

Then he remembered tales of the Little Men, who lived far in the south after the Burning Time. It was said that some Tribes had made friends with them, although no one living had ever met a man from one of those Tribes—or one of the Little Men, either. To be sure, the Little Men had been covered with fur, not feathers. But perhaps the tales did not tell everything about them?

Yes. It made sense. This was a man from the lost Tribes. He and the Little Man had come north, seeking—what? Impossible to guess. At least they had not killed him as he lay helpless.

The warrior's ears were sharp enough to catch Shangbari's sigh of relief. He looked at the hunter and smiled. "So you're awake. I'm sorry I hit you so hard, but I was in a hurry. I didn't want you to call for help." From the man's speech, he seemed to have learned the True Tongue in Kaldak.

"You have honor, then, to fight one against one?" If he did not, then Shangbari would have to force the man to kill him quickly.

"I have that honor. I also have no wish to fight you at all, without reason." That made sense, if he was seeking a new home in the north. Or perhaps his Tribe was so weak that his chief had sent him out with orders like Ikhnan's, not to fight unless there was good cause. Then for the first time the man seemed to notice Shangbari's ears.

"Do all your people have ears like yours?"

Shangbari had to laugh, and wiggled them. "Many, at least."

"Does your chief have them?"

Shangbari frowned. He did not understand what the man wanted, but so far the questions were not dishonorable. He nodded.

"And is your chief a young man, about twenty years old, with a wife and a baby?"

Again Shangbari thought of wizardry, and his frown deepened. There was still no dishonor, but could the warrior or the Little Man be drawing his thoughts from his head? Finally he nodded again.

"I hoped so. And did your chief once call himself a friend to the Seekers of Doimar, until a night when the Kaldakans came out of the sky to attack the Seekers? On that night, did not a warrior of Kaldak spare your chief and his wife and child, and tell them to flee because this was not their fight?"

Shangbari could barely breathe. Either his mind was being torn open by wizardry, or this warrior was nothing which any of the Tribes had any name for. No one outside the Red Cats—and only a few of them—knew the whole tale of the Night of the Seekers' Death. It was that Night which later brought the Doimari sky-killers, and broke forever the peace between the Red Cats and Doimar. Indeed, the men of Doimar were now greater enemies than those of Kaldak, until the blood debt was paid—if it ever was. Could this man have knowledge which would help the Red Cats pay that debt?

Shargbari decided he should lead this man to Ikhnan. This was a chief's and Grandfathers' matter, not one for even the finest hunter.

The man picked up Shangbari's rifle. "I want to go to your chief. I have things to say he must hear, and soon. If you will swear the most sacred oath you know, not to harm me or lead me astray, I will give you back your weapon. Two guns are always better than one, and also two sets of eyes."

He spoke like an experienced warrior, and Shangbari saw no reason to doubt that he was one. "By the spirits of my prey, the true shooting of my rifle, and
144

my faith in the hunter's oath, I swear to guard you as I would my brother, until you have said all that you have to say to Ikhnan, Chief of the Red Cats," Shangbari replied.

The Little Man jumped up and down, clapping his hands and going *yeep-yeep-yeep* as though he understood and approved. With a City knife, the warrior cut Shangbari's bonds, then pulled him to his feet with one hand and gave him his rifle with the other.

"Do you wish more beer?" said Ikhnan.

Blade shook his head. He'd already drunk more than enough of the rough Tribal beer while telling Ikhnan his tale. "You have already done far more than the Laws for welcoming guests demanded of you."

Ikhnan smiled grimly. "But not as much as you could have wished, or perhaps expected?"

"You are a wise leader of your people," said Blade with a shrug. "You would be wiser if you believed me more."

"That I doubt," said Ikhnan. "Though you say you did not join the sky-riders of Kaldak of your own will, yet you came among us as one of them."

"I did. And I did little harm to your people, and much to the Doimari, who are the enemies of everyone except themselves."

"That is so. But that only gives me a reason to let you return to Kaldak with your tale. It does not give me reason to let the remaining warriors of the Red Cats follow you into the jaws of the Seekers."

Blade was annoyed enough to think of several things it wouldn't be wise to say out loud. Perhaps he should give up and accept Ikhnan's offer of a guide to the Kaldakan border. That would save him a few days in getting back. Would that be enough if it took him weeks to convince the Kaldakans they should act? "Cadet Commander Voros" was probably under sentence of death for six or seven different crimes.

He would even need some luck to escape being shot on sight.

Then he heard a familiar *yeeeeping* behind him, the scrabble of Cheeky's paws, and the *pad-pad-pad* of some other animal about the same size. Ikhnan's eyes opened wide and his mouth opened wider, as he looked past Blade. Blade turned around, to see Cheeky walking into the tent with one of the sacred Red Cats following respectfully behind him. They sat down, Cheeky scratched the Red Cat behind its ears, and the beast started to purr!

Blade reached out a hand to pet the cat—and got bloody claw marks on his wrist for his pains. Then Cheeky *yeeeeped* angrily, jumped up and down, and pulled the Red Cat's tail hard. It laid its ears back, and for a moment Blade thought he would have to rescue Cheeky. The Red Cats had ferocious tempers, and this one was nearly as big as Cheeky.

The Red Cat and Cheeky glared at each other for a moment. Then slowly the Red Cat relaxed. A moment later it went over to Blade and licked the blood off his wrist, purring like a small outboard motor. Then, while Ikhnan looked as if his eyes were going to fall out of their sockets, the Red Cat climbed onto Blade's lap, curled its tail around itself, and went to sleep. Cheeky gave a small *yeeep* of satisfaction and hopped up onto Blade's shoulder.

With a heroic effort at self-control, Ikhnan spoke. "Is that Fija?"

Blade grinned. "How should I know? Ask Cheeky."

Ikhnan swallowed. "You said that as if—he might answer—like a man. Is he—?"

"He is not one of the Little Men of the tales I have heard here in the Land," said Blade. "That I can swear. As to what else he is—much I do not know myself, and most of the rest is not my secret but his."

Ikhnan swallowed again. "I am sorry to seem—less than a warrior—before you. But—"

Blade waved away the apologies. "I myself have soiled my breeches, facing what I did not under-

146

stand. Suppose you tell me what makes you uneasy. Then I will know what questions of yours I can answer."

Ikhnan nodded. "It is simply that Fija is the most evil-tempered of all the Red Cats. It is as if he wanted to feed on human flesh all the year around. No other man has been able to touch Fija without being clawed or sometimes bitten. As for his being a friend of any other living creature—I am not yet sure that what I saw was really what happened."

"I didn't know that about Fija. But Cheeky—well, he's a friendly little chap. He probably convinced Fija that he was no rival for food or females. Then it wasn't hard to persuade him that any friend of Cheeky's also ought to be a friend of Fija's."

"You said that as if you believed it. . . . No, I am sorry. Forgive me for seeming to doubt your word, as I have doubted my own eyes." Ikhnan smiled thinly. "Still, I will not trust the—Cheeky's powers enough to pet Fija myself, even if I do become your friend."

Ikhnan looked embarrassed. "Cheeky's friendship with Fija is a sign that I must do more than I would before. Yet—I still cannot simply arm my warriors and send them against Doimar at your word." He straightened up. "Voros. If you were among the sky-riders of Kaldak, you must have had friends there. Perhaps even friends among their chiefs?"

"Yes. Have you heard of a Monitor Bekror?"

Ikhnan jumped. "His land begins not more than four days from where we sit. But—he is one of the mightest enemies the Tribes have. No friendship for you would—"

"That remains to be seen. He is no friend to the Tribes, but he is a friend to me. He is also an enemy of my enemies in Kaldak. To spite them, he might even be willing to aid Tribesmen who were not going to fight him. Do you think I can ask you not to use any aid you get from Bekror against anyone except Doimar? I have *told* you several times that Doimar is

147

now a greater enemy to the Tribes than Kaldak has ever dreamed of being!"

"And I believe you. Now. But what I believe does not matter. Without some help from someone, the Red Cats *cannot* do as you wish. We had five hundred warriors. Now we have less than two hundred, and fewer than that with weapons fit to use against Doimar. If I send half my warriors with you and they do not return, the Red Cats will be too weak to stand against *anyone*. It would not matter who slew them. The Tribe would die, to the last infant."

Blade was silent. Ikhnan was a proud warrior confessing weakness, and could do without pointless remarks for a while.

Finally Blade said, "I would not ask that. It is something no honorable man could ask."

"Thank you." Ikhnan swallowed more beer, which seemed to clear his head. "I and five other warriors will travel with you to the house of Monitor Bekror. You and he shall speak. If he offers us weapons to use against Doimar, I shall swear by anything he asks not to use them against him. Will he find that just?"

Bekror would, if he believed Blade at all. If he didn't, there wasn't much Blade could do about it. He and the Tribesmen could hardly steal enough Newtec or Oltec gear to make Ikhnan willing to send his warriors against the rocket base.

Then Blade would have to convince someone else in Kaldak, if he wanted to smash Detcharn's schemes before they literally got off the ground. He would also have to do it fast, or even the serum formula wouldn't be in Kaldakan hands fast enough to do any good!

Chapter 20

The Sky Master's daughter Baliza closed the door behind her and looked across the tapestry-hung room to the great bed. Monitor Bekror was already in it, propped up on a stack of pillows. He had a book in his lap and a jug of beer with two cups on the carved wooden table beside the bed. He looked as if he might be dozing, but Baliza knew that appearances could deceive.

She locked the door, snuffed out all the lamps except the one by the bed, and started undressing. She took her time about it, since the night was warm, and there was no great hurry to get under the blankets and into Bekror's arms. Also, he said he liked to watch her slowly stripping herself down from a soldier into a love-goddess.

The first time she'd come to him, she'd thought he might have been flattering her, when all he really needed was the extra time to become aroused. After all, he would never see fifty again. Now she knew that when he said she was a work of art, he was simply telling the truth as he saw it.

When she was naked, she padded across to the bed. Bekror handed her a full cup of beer. As she drank she suddenly felt his hand between her thighs, where it tickled most. She jumped and spilled half the beer over her shoulders and breasts. Bekror sat up and started licking the beer off her skin. As his lips closed around her nipples, she put down the cup
149

and wound her fingers in his hair to pull his head against her breasts. Meanwhile his hand was still busy between her thighs, doing more than tickling.

At last she had to pull free, sweep the blankets aside, and scramble into bed. As Bekror's arms went around her, she let desire fill her and let out a soft moan of anticipation. Perhaps Bekror was not everything he'd been as a young man. But in the time since he'd been a young man he must have bedded a great many women. The women had taught him much, and he remembered all of it.

He didn't even mind the fact that she was taller and probably stronger than he was. "More to get a good hold on," was the way he put it.

She had been instructed by Geyrma to come to Sclathdan to get to the bottom of the rumors that Bekror was forming an alliance with the Tribesmen.

Now she was really beginning to feel slightly guilty about being here under an assumed name, as a representative from the City of Kaldak, supposedly inspecting his weapons. This in spite of the fact that he was obviously playing a few little games of his own. The games they played in bed were getting through to her, though, making her feel more like a woman than she had in years.

But then, perhaps he was bedding her only because he hoped this would shut her mouth? Perhaps if he knew who she really was he wouldn't have touched her. Perhaps—

Then he was in her, and she was getting all his strength and vigor. There was no "perhaps" about that, or any more thinking to be done. She wrapped her legs and arms around him, not worried about her strength if he wasn't, and he gasped with the effort he was making but smiled while he made it. . . .

There was sweat mixed with the beer on her breasts and all down her body before the loving was ended. Then Bekror seemed to fall asleep beside her, one arm flung across her breasts. She could tell that he

150

was pretending. So it might be tonight, that meeting with the Tribesmen he had planned? She decided to pretend to be asleep also, although she wanted to pull his arm more tightly across her breasts. She was getting used to having someone in bed with her. She would not find it so easily, certainly not from such a good man, when she returned to Kaldak.

At last Bekror seemed satisfied that the woman beside him was too soundly asleep to notice anything. He slipped out of bed, pulled on his clothes, and picked up pack, helmet, and rifle from the closet. When he went out, Baliza heard someone talking to him in the hallway leading to the stairs. From the few words they exchanged, it sounded like a woman. Probably Sparra, Chyatho's widow and Voros's lover.

Baliza waited another minute, then sprang out of bed, pulled on her clothes, and ran to the window. The vine below the window wasn't quite equal to her weight and gave way when she was halfway down. Lovemaking hadn't affected her trained reflexes, though—she landed with no harm and with hardly any noise. It didn't take her long to be sure no one had detected her, or to find the trail of Bekror and Sparra. She checked her weapons—the compact ten-shot laser, the loop of wire, the knives—then set off after the Monitor and his companion. She just prayed Bekror was not engaging in any treachery. She had come to care for him so much that it would be difficult to kill him.

Blade wasn't entirely surprised at Monitor Bekror's coming to the rendezvous. He'd worded his message carefully, promising that Bekror would have a marvelous chance both to help Kaldak and yet to increase his independence from the City at a very small price. Blade was still happy and relieved to see the other man appear. Any other way of getting Kaldakan help for his plans would still take time they might not have.

Bekror stepped out of the darkness, with Sparra

151

close beside him, her pistol drawn. Blade's keen night vision made out another man lurking in the bushes. After a moment, he recognized Sparra's friend, Terbo.

"Well, I'll be—!" Bekror roared. Then he remembered where he was. "It *is* Voros. And what in the name of the Lords is that on your shoulder."

"Alive and well," said Blade. "And *he* is Cheeky. Hello, Sparra."

"Hello, Voros. And—hello, Cheeky."

"*Yeeeep!*"

Blade opened his belt pouch and held out a package sealed in oiled leather. "Take this, Bekror. No matter what else happens, if it gets to Kaldak quickly there is hope for this—for everyone here." He'd nearly slipped and said "this Dimension." He wasn't quite as calm as he thought he was.

"What is it?"

"The formula for the serum against the fever the Seeker Detcharn plans to unleash on Kaldak and the Tribes."

"Voros, have you brought me out here to listen to drunken jokes? Or is this a—?"

Sparra laid a hand on his arm. "We do not have that much time we can safely spend out here. If you keep interrupting Voros, it will be the same as not letting him tell his story at all. Can we be sure it is not worth hearing?"

Bekror muttered something which Blade decided to take as an agreement. He told the whole story of what he'd done since he left the Monitor's estate. He concentrated on his adventures in Doimar, leaving out nothing except the discovery of his identity by Moshra's telepathy.

At last he introduced Ikhnan. The chief stepped forward, both hands raised in the gesture of peace. Blade could tell he was uneasy, and hoped none of the Tribesmen covering him were trigger-happy.

"I swear by the Laws of the Cities and by the weapons of my own Tribe that Voros speaks with my voice in all these things. I will take the oath he has

152

promised, if you will give us the arms we need to strike at those who are the enemies of all true men."

Ikhnan delivered the speech without a moment's hesitation or a missed word. Blade remembered that the chief was nearly young enough to be his own son. In another ten years, Ikhnan might be the man Kaldak had always feared, the chief who would unite the Tribes. Would Bekror see that possibility, too, and would it make him refuse to aid the man?

The silence dragged on. Blade thought he heard a twig snap in the distance, but the wind was rising so it was hard to tell.

Finally Bekror nodded. "I can manage the lasers and grenades. I think I'll also be able to come up with a lifter when you need it. Two, if I can. But the explosives—I don't have all you need on hand. Also, I'm not happy about letting them out of my hands even if I had them. Ikhnan, will you let me send a few of my fighters among your Tribe, to watch the explosives?"

"Do you doubt my word?"

"I do not. Nor do I doubt the word of all those fighters who follow you. But what of other Tribes? What if they decide to attack the Red Cats to seize this rich prize? You cannot have so many warriors left that you would not welcome help in defending the explosives?"

Blade and Ikhnan looked at each other. They hadn't told Bekror about the weakness of the Red Cats. Their look said as plainly as words: *This man is too shrewd for our comfort. What choice is there, but to give him what he wants?*

"It shall be as you wish," said Ikhnan. "But let the men be brave and wise enough to honor the customs of the Red Cats. Otherwise, I will swear no oath to treat them as friends, for they will not be such."

Bekror shrugged. "I will accept those terms. Sparra, would you like to be chief guard of the explosives? You can pick your own people. Anyone except—"

Blade held up a hand for silence. Over the rising

153

wind, he'd unmistakably heard sounds which shouldn't have been there. Twigs snapping, a bush rustling, something like a human cough. He started to draw his pistol.

Before it cleared the holster, the night erupted in a confusion of shouts, screams, and laser beams blazing green.

Baliza had no trouble following Bekror and Sparra in the darkness. But then, she'd never found it hard to follow people who weren't expecting to be followed. Those who'd taught her the arts of tracking thought that was a game for not very bright children.

What she overheard made her realize just what Bekror was up to, and she was so relieved she almost shouted out for joy. Clearly, Bekror and the Tribesman had formed an alliance to defeat the scheming Doimari, and this news would be very welcome back in Kaldak.

After a while, she began to think of revealing herself to the people ahead. The danger was no longer being seen. If they detected her presence, they would go after her, and it might be hard to explain just what she was doing spying on them.

Baliza was starting to approach when she realized she wasn't the only one who had followed the Monitor. She let the others get closer, and they passed without noticing her, making a good deal of noise. She knew they'd have had no chance of successfully trailing anyone who was on the alert. She also recognized enough voices to know who they were.

Chyatho's friends were on the prowl, for Sparra and perhaps for Bekror. They wanted the woman who'd betrayed their friend; perhaps they also wanted the Monitor who made life hard for New Law men whenever he could. Apart from her own preference for the Old Law, Baliza now knew that Bekror's death would be a disaster for this part of the frontier.

"People, you're dead," Baliza whispered to the night. She felt confidence and skill flowing from her mind

154

into every muscle and each limb. Was this the way her father had felt, those times he seemed to become a killer as deadly as any Fighting Machine and far more intelligent?

The amount of noise they were making let Baliza get close to the men. She counted seven, which was long odds for her to face single-handed. However, if she spoiled their surprise, Bekror and Sparra would have time to fight back. Neither of them would be an easy victim.

At last the men ahead stopped and split into two groups. Four got ready to do the actual killing while three stood guard. A very sloppy guard, Baliza thought as she slipped off her boots.

Her bare feet made no sound on the soft earth and fallen needles as she came up behind the first guard. Her fingers wound themselves in his hair and her knife slashed his throat before he knew there was anyone near. She lowered him to the ground, waited to see if his mates were alerted, then quickly searched his body for usable weapons. She found a grenade and was picking it up, when a laser beam seared past her right shoulder.

Instantly she threw herself down and to the left, rolling the moment she hit the ground. Her hand dove into her jacket pocket and came out with her own laser. It was useless beyond fifty feet, but the other two sentries were more than close enough. She shot one in the head. The other dodged behind a bush. She got ready to throw the grenade, but the sentry's laser burned her wrist and she dropped it. Fortunately the pin was still in.

She rolled again, expecting the sentry's next shot to hit or one of the other four to notice her. But suddenly the other four were fighting their own battle. She heard a sudden uproar of human voices, the crackle of several lasers, a grenade explosion, and a scream of agony. Then the last sentry was coming at her. Whether he was attacking or trying to flee she didn't know. Her legs swung, knocking him

155

down, then she threw her full weight on his back. Her knees drove into his spine and he went limp. Not waiting to see if he was dead or not, she jumped up and ran, swerving randomly from left to right and back again to make her trail hard to follow.

She had to get clear and think about what she'd seen and what it could mean. The fight around Bekror had given enough light to let her see everyone involved. Several of them *were* unmistakably Tribesmen, one of them a chief. Another was the man who'd called himself Voros.

When the fight started, Blade shouted to Sparra and Bekror, "Get down! They're probably after you!"

Instead Bekror shoved Sparra violently to the ground and opened up with his laser pistol. He didn't hit anyone, but he did set a bush on fire. The light confused the attackers, who'd been expecting a fight in the dark. Blade counted four enemies and immediately picked off one with a snap shot from the hip.

Then he himself had to flatten on the ground as the Tribesmen and Ikhnan opened a wild fire. Blade saw the three attackers go down, and also the flashes and moving shapes of something going on behind them. Their rear-guard was having its own fight.

One of the attackers threw a grenade as he went down. Blade saw it arch out into the open and land, fuse sputtering, six feet away. He knew that Bekror and Sparra would die if it exploded. He also knew the only way to keep this from happening.

Then a Tribesman hurled himself out of the darkness, landing on top of the grenade. A moment later it exploded harmlessly—except to the man on top of it.

Half-deafened, Blade rose to his feet as the Tribesman started to scream. Then he shot the man in the back of the head. There was no point in trying to cure such a wound, or even turn him over. Blade had seen what happens to a man who smothered a grenade with his own body. A quick death was all he

156

could give to the man who'd saved Bekror, Sparra—and himself, because he'd been about to leap on the grenade when the Tribesman did it.

Then there was silence, except for the crackle of the blazing bush and the distant moan of a dying man. Sparra and Terbo went off to investigate, and came back a couple of minutes later, looking grim.

"One of their sentries, with his back broken," she said. "He admitted they were Chyatho's friends out to kill me and Bekror. Said, 'We'd have done it without that big bitch.'"

"Big bitch?" repeated Bekror. He looked startled, then hastily straightened his face.

"That's what he said. Then he died."

"No loss," said Bekror evenly.

"N-n-no," said Sparra. She was obviously fighting off the shakes, frightened over the night's events, even more frightened of appearing a coward in the eyes of the Tribesmen.

"They were not men the gods could love," said Ikhnan. "The Laws of the Cities are not ours. But men who will kill because they are not allowed to defy a Law are evil anywhere." He looked down at the dead Tribesman. "I only wish he had died against a worthier foe."

"He died well, nonetheless," said Bekror. He picked up two of the dead man's guns and handed them to Ikhnan. "For his grave."

Ikhnan's eyes widened. "You know our custom, of putting the weapons of a slain warrior's enemies on his grave?"

"Of course," said Bekror. "I have long been the enemy of the Tribes. I may be the enemy of the Tribes again. I have never been, and never will be, ignorant of their ways." In the silence these words produced, he went on:

"Indeed, I would propose that we bury him here and now, with both peoples doing him honor. However, we are too close to my lands. Someone without respect for the dead might pollute his grave."

"If we're that close to your lands, shall we finish our talking before we have more unwelcome visitors?" said Blade. "The best honor we can do for this warrior is not to let his death be wasted."

No one disagreed, and the negotiations were finished quickly. A lifter would deliver Sparra and her squad with the weapons and explosives to an agreed-on rendezvous in five days. When Bekror got more explosives, he would deliver them along with the lifters themselves, when the raiders were ready to move out.

Then Bekror's party vanished, leaving the Tribesmen and Blade to pick up their dead and retreat. "A wise and mighty chief," Ikhnan called Bekror. He called him other things, too, but Blade was too absorbed in his own thoughts to remember any of them.

What had happened in the fight with the would-be assassins' sentries? And who was the "big bitch"? Bekror knew, at least, or thought he knew. If he didn't, Blade was no judge of faces or voices!

Blade had a nasty feeling that there were going to be other players in this game he'd begun—players he hadn't asked to sit in, and who might reveal themselves only when it was too late to change the rules.

Chapter 21

"You're absolutely sure it was Voros himself?" said Geyrna. "You only saw him once, in poor light, and in a hurry."

"I'm sure, Aunt," said Baliza. "Between what I saw and what I wormed out of Bekror, it couldn't be anybody else. Unless you think it's my father the Sky Master Blade come back again? She laughed and stretched catlike. It felt fine to be safe at home in Kaldak again, able to relax and soak up the sun and good food. It wasn't going to last very long, though.

"You *almost* said that as if it was a joke," said Geyrna. Baliza felt her face going hot, but her aunt didn't seem to notice as she went on. "Certainly Voros seems to be almost as good a fighter and leader as the Sky Master. He also seems to have the same gift for talking sense and making you realize it. I can't imagine he would have impressed that stubborn old cynic Bekror otherwise. By the way, how was he?"

Baliza couldn't quite suppress a pleasurable wriggle at the memories. Her aunt laughed. "Still good, eh? I had him a few years ago myself, and I couldn't complain either."

A servant came in with beer and snacks, interrupting the flow of bawdy chatter. When the two women were alone again, Geyrna got down to business.

"So now we know Bekror and the Tribesmen intend to launch a major strike at Detcharn's rockets.

159

If it's true Voros is among them, we can be sure the training of the Tribesmen is in good hands.

"But that may not be enough. With what he'll have, Voros can only take thirty, maybe forty men, to *near* the base. They'll have to walk the rest of the way. Suppose he had two or three real Doimari lifters, such as the ones we've captured in past wars? Suppose he could take sixty or eighty men in those lifters all the way to the rocket base before anyone there knew anything was wrong? And suppose, also, men were sent from the City Regiment to help Voros?"

Baliza's eyes widened. "Of course. I should have thought of that myself. Aunt, you wouldn't be such a bad soldier yourself."

"Thank you. But I had good teachers, like Sidas. I listened to everyone who ever talked about war while I was around."

"You also heard some wise words from Bairam," said Kareena.

Geyrna frowned. "Not *his* wisdom, I think. More likely what he heard from the Sky Master and passed on."

"You do him an injustice, I think."

"You would say that even if you didn't think it, just to annoy me."

"If more people had said it to you twenty years ago, Bairam might not have started drinking."

"He started drinking because I would not stay fifteen years old forever. That was what he loved, not the woman who knew she could do better at ruling Kaldak than he."

Baliza sighed. It was an old and bitter quarrel between them, and right now even more pointless than usual. "Forgive me, Aunt. But you know what I have thought on this for so many years. I keep hoping that one day you'll listen."

"Perhaps I will, one day. Certainly not before we've stamped Detcharn and his plans into the ground." She sipped her beer. "But let's be serious again. To

160

get those Doimari lifters and additional men, we're going to have to go to Sidas."

"So?"

"Sidas is a hard-headed son of a munfan, as you should know. Sidas is also very shrewd, and he's going to notice you're full of thoughts you won't confess, about this mysterious Voros. He may ask questions. When he does, you'd better be ready to tell him the truth, or as much of it as you know yourself."

"I'll do my best."

"Your best had better be pretty damned good, Baliza!"

"You next, Shangbari," the woman Sparra said.

Shangbari lay down, his fire rifle pointing out in front of him. It was strange, obeying a woman so easily. But it no longer seemed un-Lawful. Voros followed the Laws of the Cities, which said that women might be warriors and hunters; Shangbari had sworn to follow Voros.

Some of the warriors of the Red Cats had still been stupid enough to think that Sparra was a woman for bedding, in spite of their oaths. Some of those would not be thinking of women for many days—or at least thinking would be all they could do. Sparra had done the work on them herself, too. She'd said that Voros taught her those ways of fighting.

Was there anything about war Voros did not know or could not teach? Shangbari doubted it. Certainly he did not wonder that the Red Cats were beginning to call the new leader "Voros the Wise."

"All right, Shangbari," Sparra said. "This is an Oltec rifle. Remember, it shoots burning hot light, not single bullets. You must take your finger off the trigger the moment you hit the target. Otherwise the rifle will lose its magic too quickly."

"I understand." He'd begun to understand more than he wanted to admit to this woman or even to Voros. Among the things he'd begun to understand

161

was that there was no magic in Oltec. If you had the right tools and knew how to use them, it was no harder to make one of the "magic" rifles than it was to tan a hide or sharpen a spear.

Someday the Tribes would have those tools and know how to make their own rifles. Then they could avenge their dead on all the Cities. But—if there were people in the Cities like Voros and Sparra—yes, and Bekror—might there not be peace someday between Tribe and City?

That thought was so new and frightening that Shangbari had to grip his rifle more tightly than ever. He did not want Sparra to see his hands shaking, or miss his target.

He was ready to shoot again, when suddenly a City sky-machine passed over the clearing. A moment later if floated down to a landing place on the other side of the little stream which divided the clearing. All the men practicing with the rifles jumped up and shouted. Sparra was shouting, too. She seemed angry that the men would not listen to her. Then she saw Voros himself walking toward the machine, and shrugged.

"All right. It's pretty late anyway."

By the time Shangbari reached the machine, the City men in it were unloading boxes. Voros counted them as they came out. Shangbari recognized the writing on some of the boxes. They held the "explosives" which they would use to destroy the Doimari machines.

Now a big man in City clothing stepped out of the sky-machine. "Hoy, Voros!" he shouted.

Voros turned. "What the—?" Ezarn?"

"Have you ever met anybody else as big and smelly, old friend?" He stepped up to Voros and gripped him by both shoulders. "How's the work here, Voros? Got enough to give me some?"

"You can stay?"

"If you'll have me."

"Will I have you? Does rain fall down, or smoke
162

rise? Come and have a beer. It's the Tribal brew, I'm afraid, but—"

"Won't need to drink that tonight, Voros. I came with a barrel of my own from Bekror's."

"Even better."

The two big men walked off side by side. Shangbari wondered who the new man, Ezarn, was. Obviously a City warrior, and he looked like a good one who would make the attack on the Doimari much stronger. He'd also greeted Voros as though they were sworn brothers or at least old battle-mates.

Then why did Voros look and speak as though he did not understand Ezarn's coming, or even feared it?

Outside the hut it was dark. Blade piled more wood on the fire and rolled the empty beer barrel out of the way. Sparra was already asleep under the furs in the corner. Cheeky was curling up in the crook of her arm, not only asleep but snoring.

"So, old friend," said Blade. "What really brought you out here—besides Bekror's lifter, that is?"

Ezarn had either drunk enough to slow his thoughts, which weren't too fast to begin with, or else he was picking his words with care. "When I got back from leave, they asked me to come out here. Well, they really asked me if I'd go out to Bekror's, to help train his men. I'd get regular pay, and maybe more than that from Bekror."

"Who asked?"

"The High Commander Sidas."

"He asked, not ordered?"

"Couldn't say. But then, you know him. Could *you* tell if he was being nice or giving an order?" Ezarn had a point there. So why was Blade thinking that "couldn't say" might have a double meaning?

"I couldn't refuse," Ezarn went on. He hiccupped. "So I came out, and Bekror tells me about you and the friendly Tribesmen. Are their women friendly, too? You've got your own, I see," he said with a wave at Sparra.

"If you're a friend of Voros and observe their customs—yes, the women are friendly enough."

"Good. Real good." Ezarn cocked his head on one side, as if he was thinking hard. His head stayed at that angle, then Blade heard a long rumbling snore. The beer had finally got to him.

Blade got up and arranged Ezarn so he could sleep comfortably in the chair. Then he barred the hut door, pulled off his clothes and crawled in under the furs beside Sparra. She murmured contentedly as she felt him beside her, and pressed one firm breast against his arm. Cheeky went right on sleeping—but then, he could sleep through an earthquake if he wanted to.

Blade's feeling that somebody he didn't know was taking a hand in the game was stronger than ever. Or maybe several somebodies? It was no worse than usual in the secret-operations business, but that didn't mean he had to like it!

Ezarn's coming out here was a good sign, though. Nobody who knew much about the big soldier would send him on any mission dangerous to "Voros." Anybody who didn't know Ezarn's loyalty was too stupid to be very dangerous, *whatever* they wanted.

Chapter 22

Baliza wondered why High Commander Sidas had invited her and Geyrna to his house outside Kaldak. Didn't he trust the people in his office anymore? At least it got her and her aunt a good dinner—Sidas's cook was famous all over Kaldak.

In his private chamber afterward, Sidas served sweet wine and dismissed the servants. Then he locked the door after them. When he turned back to his guests, his face was suddenly much harder. Baliza was now almost certain that he disapproved of their plan—which they had told him about earlier at his headquarters—to send Doimari lifters to Voros. Sidas probably invited them to his house to tell them so. He probably also had some other things to discuss, and Baliza feared it had something to do with Voros.

Then Sidas sat down on the corner of the great wooden table by the wall, one booted leg crossed over the other. "So you want me to send Voros two or three of our Doimari lifters, do you? Why?"

His sharp tone stung Baliza. "We've already explained why."

"Tell me again."

"Very well, then. The three Doimari lifters can take twice as many men and guns as Bekror's two. Voros will have a stronger force, and he can fly it right into the base. With surprise on his side, he'll do more damage, then get more of his men out again."

"Maybe. You have a lot of faith in Voros."

"Yes. Don't you?"

"Not that much. I would believe the Sky Master Blade could do something like this. Not Voros, a man from nowhere. He's a good soldier, I'll admit. Maybe one of our best, and I don't really doubt his loyalty, even if he did desert after the rape charge. But I don't think he's good enough to do this, and with Tribesmen."

Sidas's eyes were like stones now as he lit a cigar and offered them to the women. Geyrna took one. Baliza refused. She was afraid her hands would shake if she reached for it. Sidas puffed quietly for a minute or so, then stabbed at Baliza with the cigar.

"I'll give Voros the lifters, under one condition. You tell me the truth. Who do you think he *really* is?"

For a moment Baliza thought she was going to be sick. Then the nausea passed and relief took its place. The question she'd feared for so long had been asked, and she was still alive.

"I think Voros is my father, the Sky Master Blade, returned to Kaldak. I do not know how he did this, but I think he has."

"Never mind how he got back here—at least for now," Sidas added. "Tell me how you decided he was—who he is." Baliza was glad to notice the hesitation in Sidas's voice. The idea of the Sky Master Blade among them again had slightly shaken even the iron-nerved High Commander.

So Baliza told Sidas and Geyrna everything she'd learned or thought about the man who called himself Voros. She kept her voice clear and steady, even through the tale of the night she'd tried to seduce him, although she felt her face turning red. Sidas was obviously trying not to laugh, but only said, "I always thought that warm blood of yours would get you into trouble one of these days. Well, better to be the way you are and your mother was, then cold and alone." Then he was silent until she'd finished, when

166

he handed her another glass of wine. She emptied it quickly.

Sidas sat with his hands folded in his lap, his cigar burning itself out unnoticed, until she was finished. Then:

"I'm glad you told the truth," he said. "I wouldn't have held back the lifters, no matter what. In fact, I've already decided to send the lifters. You see, Bekror sent me a serum formula given him by Voros. I had the formula studied by a few of our own people. They say Voros is telling the truth: it is indeed an antidote to the deadly germs Detcharn plans to let loose on Kaldak. So Veros has gotten all the help I can give him, no matter who he is."

"You won't send people from—oh, the City Regiment? Wouldn't they do the job better than raw Tribesmen?"

"With the best weapons and Voros-Blade to lead them, those 'raw Tribesmen' will be good enough. Also, City people wouldn't follow Voros unless he was pardoned for his desertion. That would raise a lot of questions better left lying. If it *is* Blade come back, he's probably got good reasons for not wanting everybody knowing it. For the time being, I'll respect those reasons, though I did decide to send one man from the City Regiment to help Voros train his men."

Sidas lit another cigar, and this time Baliza joined him, although she put hers down after a few puffs. She was afraid she would be sick all over again. "No, what I'd have done if you'd lied wouldn't hurt Voros. I'd simply have ordered you to sit in Kaldak during this fight. Under arrest, if necessary." She could tell he wasn't joking.

"Then—I can join my—Voros—in the raid on the rocket base?" She hadn't realized until now just how badly she wanted to do this, and she still didn't know exactly why.

Sidas shook his head. "He's too likely to recognize you, and spend time worrying about keeping you out of danger. That's not a worry to give a man

167

leading a raid like that. I know," he said with a sigh. "Your mother, as much as I loved her, would never stop giving me that worry."

"But if he's not my father—"

"Even if he really *is* just a man named Voros, it's still not a good idea. Do you think he'll want to be remembered as the man who led the Sky Master Blade's daughter to her death?"

Baliza had no answer to that question, then decided there wasn't any. "Very well. You're right. But—the Laws abandon me if I'm just going to sit on my bottom in Kaldak while this is happening! You will have to put me under arrest to make me do it, I warn you!"

"I don't expect you to do anything of the sort!" said the High Commander. "In fact, we've got work for you every bit as important as the raid. You're going to enter Doimar and bring out Feragga."

Baliza must have looked as confused as she felt, because Sidas explained himself very carefully. Baliza was to enter Doimar, find out where Feragga lived, go there, and bring her to Kaldak. Since Feragga was crippled, this would mean stealing a lifter as well.

"You should be ready to take her by force if you have to. But as the Sky Master's daughter, you're the one person in Kaldak who might not have to. That's why you're going alone. If we sent in a squad, she'd probably kill herself rather than move an inch."

"Assuming she comes to Kaldak of her own free will, what then?"

"A lot of Detcharn's enemies will rally around her if she's alive after the raid. She won't be if we don't get her out of Doimar. Detcharn will kill her if he survives the raid, and his friends will try if he doesn't. With luck, Feragga will be ruler of Doimar again."

"It will take more than luck," said Baliza. "It will take the consent of the Council of Nine."

For the first time, Geyrna spoke. "I think that will

not be such a problem as you might think." Something in her voice . . .

"You two worked this out between you," Baliza exclaimed. "You—you've been playing with me all this time!"

Sidas tried to look ashamed. He wasn't very successful. As angry as she was, Baliza wanted to laugh. Finally she said, "All right. Feragga will make a good rallying point. Even if she doesn't, she shouldn't die at the hands of Detcharn's hired killers. I'll go, on one condition."

"Yes?" said the other two, almost in unison.

"If I don't come back, if Voros returns, go to him and speak plainly about his secret. If he is—my father—ask him to forgive me for—what I tried to do. Tell him I honored and loved him as best I could, although not as much as he deserved."

"And if he doesn't come back?" said Sidas quietly. Baliza remembered how many people her stepfather had sent out who hadn't come back. For the first time she saw clearly that he was growing old under that burden.

"Then let him be remembered as a warrior of Kaldak. He was that, whatever else he was." They could all drink to that.

The lifter came to a stop a man's height above the ground. Baliza swung herself out the door and dropped into the long grass. She carried a heavy pack, but the grass and the damp earth made for a soft landing. She stepped out from under the lifter and waved to the two pilots. They waved back, then the lifter whined away across the field. It stayed low, and quickly vanished behind the trees dimly visible on the edge of the field.

The long grass and soft earth now made walking difficult. After a while Baliza gave up trying to avoid leaving a trail and simply plowed straight on. By the time she reached the edge of the field it was noticeably lighter. She was soaked to the skin from the waist down, and she also discovered that the grass was full of insects. She took her trousers off and picked the insects out while studying her map.

She was about two days' walk from Doimar by the shortest route, which she could not use. It brought her too close to the biggest training camp of the army of Doimar. The countryside there would be crawling with soldiers and the sky filled with lifters. So she would have to take a longer route. Call it four days' traveling. That should still get her to Doimar with plenty of time to find out where Feragga was and how to get her out of the city, before the raiders struck the rocket base. After the raid, the Doimari would be very much on the alert, not to mention quick on the trigger. Also, Feragga might be dead.

Things might go faster if she got help from the agents Kaldakan Intelligence already had in Doimar. Certainly they would have orders to do their best for her—Sidas had made that very clear.

"If they don't, I'll be asking why. And if they don't have some very good answers, they'll be envying Tribesman slaves before I get through with them." From Sidas's expression, Baliza was glad she hadn't tried to lie to him. He wasn't cruel, but he was ruthlessly just in handing out both rewards and punishments.

"The Intelligence people owe us a big debt for their clowning around. If they'd done their work properly, we'd have learned about Detcharn's fever rockets a long time ago. We wouldn't have to be throwing good men into a fangjaw's mouth to do their work for them!"

However, the fact remained that the Intelligence people certainly hadn't lived up to their name. Would they be more trouble than help, when it came to snatching Feragga?

Right now, though, she had to get to Doimar, before she even needed to worry about anything else. When she'd finished getting the insects out of her pants, Baliza pulled a set of farm woman's clothing out of her pack. Turned inside out, her pack looked just like a Doimari carrying sack. To complete her disguise, she unfolded a broad-brimmed hat. It shielded her face from the sun and prying eyes. A concealed pocket in the brim also held a miniature laser pistol, where she could easily draw it with a gesture nobody would suspect.

An hour after sunrise, two things happened at once. Baliza reached the bank of the Pesto River, and three lifters flew overhead. One of them was towing a balloon-load of troops. Before they were out of sight, Baliza saw the lifters start to circle, while the balloon began to descend.

It *might* be just a training exercise. But it looked to Baliza a lot too much like a search party. For the moment they were a long way behind her, but that might change. She had to get out of the area as fast as she could—not easy, with a river half a mile wide in front of her.

However, there were boats on rivers. Baliza started prowling along the bank, looking for an untended boat. Half an hour later she found a fisherman sitting on the bank, beside a beached canoe. He was sitting facing the river, all his attention on the dip net in his lap. He was mending its broken handle as Baliza crept up through the bushes behind him.

When she knew she hadn't been detected, she pulled out a slingshot and a handful of clay balls. Being the Sky Master's daughter gave her the chance to learn all sorts of unusual fighting skills from equally unusual teachers. She still didn't think she knew as much as her father—the tales of his bare-handed duel against the arrogant Hota still thrilled her. But she felt she'd learned enough to be a worthy daughter to the Sky Master—and would she ever have a chance to ask him if he thought so, too?

Baliza aimed the slingshot, pulled the cord back, and let fly. The clay ball took the fisherman in the temple and he toppled over sideways without even a groan. Baliza hurried out of cover and examined

171

him. The clay ball had disintegrated on impact, as it was supposed to. The fisherman himself was senseless but breathing steadily. In a few hours he would awake with a crashing headache, a blue bruise on his temple, and no memory of what happened to him. The captured Tribesmen who'd taught her to use the slingshot in return for his freedom would have been proud of her.

She dropped her pack and hat into the canoe and pushed it into the water, then climbed in. A few paddle strokes took her out into the current. Within moments she was on her way downstream toward Doimar, faster than she could have walked and with much less effort.

The morning sun blazed on the water and made the ripples sparkle like jewels. She put her hat back on but took off her shirt. She knew that a soldier who sees a good-looking woman going about bare to the waist will seldom bother to ask questions—or at least not questions about whether she's a spy.

Chapter 23

It was late afternoon, with the shadows growing long and the heat of the day beginning to die. Shangbari stretched, then rose to his feet and started walking restlessly up and down. If this had been a common hunt or raid, the men would by now have been picking up their weapons, cleansing themselves before the Grandfathers, and gathering ready to leave the camp.

Not this time, with Voros the Wise leading them against the wizards of Doimar. The sixty warriors would go aboard the sky-machines at night, fly to the wizards' home in the darkness, and attack it at dawn.

"They won't find it easy to see us on the way in," Voros had said. "By the time we've finished wrecking the place, they'll be too busy to bother us on the way out." Although Voros had also said that victory would be worth the life of every one of the raiders, he seemed determined to bring home as many men as he could.

So the raiders were facing a sleepless night and a long day. Most were sleeping or resting now. Some were with their women, including Voros himself.

Shangbari had no fit woman for this time. His first wife had died trying to give him a son. He'd been courting a second woman when the Doimari struck and she died under the fire-beams. He would shout her name as his war cry while he fought the wizards.

Still restless, he walked through the village and

around on old sow asleep in her accustomed place in the middle of the path. A hundred paces farther on, he came to the three sky-machines. They lay in the shadow of the trees, covered with branches to make them hard to see from the sky. The Doimari war colors showed faintly through the green leaves.

Shangbari was not entirely happy about going into such a great and important battle in disguise. Yet perhaps this was necessary, if you were fighting wizards. If they did not know who you were until your weapons struck them down, they could not work their magic against you.

Certainly Voros had said so, to those who not only had doubts but spoke them out loud. He'd also said that anyone who argued further would have to fight either him or his battle-brother, the Sergeant Ezarn.

No one wanted to raise a hand against Voros the Wise. The battle spirits might punish them for fighting in disguise, but they would be punished far worse for defying the spirit-blessed Voros. As for fighting Brother Ezarn—he could fight any two warriors of the Red Cats without even working up a heavy sweat. He had done so with fifty men looking on, and without breaking any law or custom of the Red Cats while doing it. No, fighting Ezarn might not be cursed, but it would certainly be very foolish.

As he got closer to the sky-machines, Shangbari saw Ezarn himself in front of one of them. He had one of their little doors open and was doing something to what lay inside with City man's tools.

"Hullo, Shangbari."

"Greetings, Ezarn. May I watch?"

"Can't sleep, hunh?"

"No."

"Neither can I. Sit yourself down, by all means."

"I thank you."

Shangbari sat down cross-legged as Ezarn used both hands to pull a length of metal tube out of the door. The hunter thought that if he watched Ezarn long enough, he might learn something about the

174

sky-machines of the Cities. The more he learned, the better. Voros, Sparra, and Ezarn did not seem to care about Tribesmen gaining such knowledge. If there was war again between the Red Cats and the Cities, everything the Red Cats learned would give them new strength.

The towers of Doimar were silhouetted against a sunset sky as Baliza turned into the Street of the Winesellers. Torches and lamps glowed all up and down the street, as the wineshops began their evening's business. Baliza's eyes turned upward, to lights on the roof of a five-story building halfway down the street. That was Feragga's city home. As long as the lights went on every night, she was living there.

A hand touched her shoulder softly and a voice murmured in her ear, "Tombs and cigars."

"Hello, Kandro," Baliza replied. She turned to see the little Intelligence agent standing behind her, munching a sausage. "Any changes?"

He shook his head. "Only two guards, and both of them half asleep already."

With only two guards, Feragga either didn't fear danger or didn't care about her life. It would be easy to get past two guards, then hold the stairs to Feragga's quarters for more than long enough. Provided, of course, that the other two Intelligence men did *their* job of stealing a lifter. . . .

"What if she won't come with you?" said Kandro softly.

"She probably will," said Baliza. "But if she won't, she won't."

"We *could* kill her," said Kandro hopefully.

"No," said Baliza sharply. They'd been over the question before. If this was the way Intelligence people thought, no wonder they hadn't discovered Detcharn's plans!

"If we kill her, we'll turn all her friends into friends of Detcharn. They'll want vengeance on Kaldak. If we leave her alive, on the other hand, it will prove again that Kaldak doesn't want war to the death."

"Perhaps." Kandro's face brightened. "Also, we will prove that we can slip into the heart of Doimar at will. They'll be sleeping lightly and looking over their shoulders for years after that."

"Right," said Baliza. She punched him in the shoulder. Kandro would see reason if you hit him over the head often enough.

The sight of the sausage in the other's hand reminded Baliza that she hadn't eaten anything since breakfast. Her stomach rumbled.

"Where did you get that sausage?"

The man pointed down the street to a shop with an open window in front. A line was forming at the window, to buy sausages, loaves of hot bread, and mugs of beer and wine.

It would not be as good as a regular meal at a table, but Baliza wanted to stay out of taverns and eating houses. In a room with only one or two doors, it was too easy to be trapped. In the streets she could run, or fight, with less risk of slaughtering half a dozen innocent Doimari.

That was something else she'd learned from her father's example and her mother's teachings—although the Lords of the Law knew Kareena had no reason to call *any* Doimari "innocent." Still, she'd been strict in what she demanded of herself and the fighters under her, as well as what she taught her daughter.

When you must kill, kill swiftly. But do not kill at all, if there is any other way of winning.

Detcharn watched the lamps coming on all over the rocket base. He went on watching until the last light was gone from the sky. He didn't need either the sun or the lamps to know where everything was. The base was his creation—a creation devoted wholly to the destruction of Kaldak and every other enemy of Doimar.

176

The Day of that destruction was coming fast. Most of the rockets for the first attack were ready in their launching tubes. All they needed was their fuel and their load of fever germs. The last rockets would be in place tomorrow. The reserve rockets were all finished and waiting in the storehouse.

The pressurized cylinders of liquid germ culture had been moved to the main guardhouse. That way there were armed men around them every minute of the day and night. The huge fuel tanks were full, ready to feed the rockets through carefully tested pipelines.

In short, everything had been done or was going to be done in time without much trouble. Detcharn could breathe easy—and also amuse himself. He rang for his servant and told the man to have the guards bring up Arsha. She was the assistant to the scientist who'd mistreated Voros's pet Cheeky. A pity Voros hadn't shot her, in addition to the scientist, although then Detcharn wouldn't be having this opportunity to punish her himself.

When the guards brought Arsha in, she had a black eye and a bleeding lip, and one shoulder of her gown was torn. Detcharn raised his eyebrows, and the guards turned pale.

"I presume she struggled?" His voice was a smooth purr.

One of the guards gave a jerky nod. "Yes. *Du-Shro*. She gave one of us a knee in the belly. A little lower, and he'd 'ave really been 'urtin. So we gave her something to remind her, not to be doin' it again."

"Very well," said Detcharn. "You were within your rights. You will hear no more of this." He looked at Arsha. "She will, however." He was glad to see her shudder in spite of the men holding her. "Now leave us."

Once he was alone with Arsha, Detcharn threw off his robe. He stood naked while the woman slowly undressed. He noted that the bruises and cuts from

177

her last visit were healing nicely; she would have her strength back.

When she was naked, Detcharn pointed at the floor in front of him. "Kneel," he said. She did not dare disobey or even be slow, but her face was twisted in shame and disgust.

Good. Serving him like this was still unpleasant for her. If she ever came to enjoy it, he would have to find some other method of continuing her punishment. Arsha hadn't yet paid in full for her stupidity over Voros and Cheeky.

As the woman's lips closed on him, Detcharn once again regretted that Voros had been killed in that lifter crash. He'd deserved a chance to help punish Arsha, too. And if Moshra hadn't died, too, maybe they'd have learned a little more about telepathy from Voros and Cheeky. Oh, well, one Kaldakan deserter more or less could hardly make that much difference.

Then Detcharn gave himself up entirely to pleasure.

Blade saw the last campfires of the Red Cats fade into the darkness behind the lifter. He saw that the other pilot had the controls, got up, and went aft. He moved cautiously, so as not to affect the machine's balance. With twenty men and all their weapons and equipment aboard, the lifter was loaded to capacity.

The cabin was dark, but the air was thick with the smells of gun oil and unwashed Tribesmen. Near the open rear hatch, the air was fresher. Blade stuck his head out briefly, saw the other two lifters were following steadily a hundred yards behind, and relaxed. It was a clear night, and if it stayed that way there would be no problem with the lifters losing each other. In fact, there wasn't a bloody thing for him to do for about the next four hours! He might as well try to get some sleep.

Normally Blade would have found it easy to do this. Once a military operation passed the point of
178

no-return, he usually found it easy to relax. Not this time. Was it the stakes being so much higher than usual—life or death for a whole Dimension—a Dimension that he himself had shaped? Was it the Dimension X secret being at stake? Or what?

A soft *yeeep* sounded at his feet. Then Cheeky hopped up on the edge of the hatch. Gently Blade took him by the scruff of the neck and put him back inside. Cheeky had insisted on coming along, the moment he knew that his master was going to war. Blade let him come, because if Blade didn't come back Cheeky wasn't likely to survive very long among the Red Cats or even on Bekror's estate. However, Blade also hoped he could be persuaded to stay inside the lifters when they reached the base. Blade would have too much else to do to spend time keeping Cheeky out of trouble.

Blade couldn't sleep, he couldn't smoke, he couldn't drink, and he couldn't pace up and down without disturbing the balance of the lifter and showing the Tribesmen that he was nervous. He couldn't talk to anyone because Ezarn was asleep and everyone else he knew was in one of the other lifters. In fact, there really wasn't a bloody thing he *could* do!

So he propped himself against the rear wall of the cabin, his rifle across his knees and his belt of power cells draped over it. He leaned back and tried to relax, even if he wasn't going to get to sleep. . . .

Half an hour later, a change of course woke Ezarn. He splashed his face with water from his canteen, then crawled off on hands and knees. He'd never liked to stand up in an airborne lifter. When he reached the rear of the cabin, he found Voros sound asleep, head sunk on his chest. Carefully Ezarn shifted him so that his neck wouldn't get twisted. You can't expect a man to lead in battle with a stiff neck!

Chapter 24

Detcharn greeted the dawn on his private balcony. He wished it was the dawn of the Day; he was getting impatient. Also, he was short of sleep. To reduce Arsha to proper submission took a while. However, he'd finally succeeded. In fact, she was now so submissive that his pleasure was shrinking. Should he declare that her punishment was over, let her return to her work, and look about for a new woman?

Perhaps. But he would do better to decide this after breakfast. He stretched, letting the dawn breeze blow across his bare chest. He wore only trousers and his weapons belt, and he wore the belt only because it would set a bad example for the guards if he didn't. Arsha was so cowed that she would hardly have dared touch his pistol or one of his knives if he'd handed it to her!

The rocket base was beginning to wake up. Tiny figures scurried along paths, and steam tractors trailed dust and smoke. Three lifters slid in over the rocket pits, heading for the main guardhouse. Detcharn saw they wore regular military markings. Probably some company out on night exercises, hoping to negotiate a free breakfast and hot showers from him. They should have given him more warning, but they'd get what they came for anyway. It never did any harm, to make the regular soldiers more grateful to the Seekers.

180

The lifters were now circling the guardhouse, as if they were asking permission to land. Detcharn was about to go inside and Sky-Voice to whatever fool of a guard commander couldn't make up his mind, when two of the lifters landed in a cloud of dust. The third stopped circling and came toward the cliff and the laboratories.

The raiders circled five times around the main guardhouse while Blade studied it to make sure there weren't any new weapons in place. All he saw was the same two lasers he'd seen while he was a prisoner.

Time to land. As Blade's two lifters settled down, Sparra's passed overhead on its way to the cliff. The men in it would blow up the heavy weapons on top of the cliff, then keep any armed Seekers or guards in the laboratories from crashing the party at the base.

The dust settled. Blade opened the door and climbed out. He wore the uniform of a Doimari rank which worked out to full colonel, so the guards at the door snapped to attention.

"Good morning, sir."

"Good morning. Call your commander. My men and I want breakfast and hot showers."

"Ah—yes, sir. Our own people are eating now, but—"

"We've been on patrol all night. Yours have spent all night in bed. Move!"

The guards decided this was the wrong time to argue. "Who shall we say is calling, sir?"

Blade took a deep breath.

"Moshra!"

Then he drew his laser and shot both men through the head.

Blade's shout of his battle cry and the shots were the signal to the other raiders. The turret-mounted laser on top of one lifter opened fire, knocking out one of the guardhouse weapons at once. Led by

Ezarn and Ikhnan, forty Tribesmen in Doimári uniforms swarmed out of both lifters.

Blade threw a grenade at the guardhouse door. It buckled the metal, but flying fragments sang past his ears. *Careful* he told himself. With vengeance for Moshra so close at hand, it would be fatally easy to get careless.

Ezarn tossed two grenades up on the roof of the guardhouse. They blew the barrel off the second laser and most of its crew off the roof. Not all of them came down in one piece.

Then suddenly the grenade-buckled main door crashed open, and the guards came swarming out. Some of them had their guns in their hands, but others were unarmed. Some were partly clothed or even entirely naked. Even the armed ones didn't shoot at Blade. He fired a couple shots, then had to jump back to avoid being trampled into the concrete. The guards seemed blind with panic.

Then the Tribesmen and the heavy laser opened up together. The Tribal marksmen took the guards in front, and the heavy laser took the ones in the rear. Blade had to duck to avoid being shot down with the guards. His hands over his ears could shut out their screams, but he couldn't shut out the smell of burning flesh and fresh blood.

When he got up, the last few surviving guards were scattering frantically, with the best marksmen among the raiders shooting at them. In front of the door was a waist-high pile of charred and mangled corpses. Blade walked toward the pile, although the stench was strong enough to turn even his iron stomach. *Something* besides the raiders had thrown the guards into a mindless panic. He had to find out what it was and if it was dangerous to his men, even if he had to plow through the sickening pile of dead.

He didn't have to go that far. Through the open door he saw a pile of shiny steel cylinders, half-covered with tarpaulins. On the cylinders he saw the familiar red coding for the fever germs. If his grenade had exploded inside instead of against the doors, and breached any of the cylinders so that concentrated culture of fever germs sprayed out under pressure . . .

He backed away so hastily that he ran into Ezarn. The big man's face turned grim as Blade explained. "No wonder they all came out from there like it was a fire up their arses," he said. "I would've been out front of all of them!"

Now that the guards were gone, however, the guardhouse made an ideal command post. With the fever culture inside, nobody would dare shoot at it. Or if they did, it would be a sign they were so desperate that the raiders were doomed anyway.

One of the lifters took off, to drop the explosives made up into bombs into the missile silos. The Tribesmen unloaded the demolition charges from the other, then Blade flew it up on to the roof. From there he could cover the Tribesmen with the turret laser, while they placed the demolition charges by the fuel dump. Blade and five Tribesmen stayed on the roof to defend the lifters.

As Ikhnan and the demolition team scurried toward the bulging mounds of the fuel tanks, Blade forced himself to appear completely calm. So far the raid was going much better than he'd expected, but he had the feeling this was the calm before the storm.

He looked up at the top of the cliff, in time to see the first of the weapons mounted there explode.

Detcharn had just stepped out on the balcony again when the explosion went off overhead. He knew it was futile to curse, but did so anyway. It was impossible for him to stand here in silence, even if he couldn't give any orders.

Whoever was leading the raid knew the base much too well. Some traitor of a Seeker, or—and his breath stopped—Voros? *Had* Voros died in that accident?

If he hadn't, and it was him leading the Tribesmen

183

and Kaldakans, that explained why the raiders were hitting the vital points. They had destroyed the operating equipment of both elevators in the laboratory complex, so nobody could get up to drive them off. And they'd smashed the Sky Voices, so Detcharn couldn't even give orders to the guards elsewhere who *could* move.

But—were the other guards still able to fight? Detcharn leaned over the railing and stared at the distant guardhouse. There wasn't nearly as much movement there as he would have expected, and a couple of lifters on the roof which shouldn't be there, and some smoke—

He'd have to get to the emergency stairs and down on the ground. Once there he could find someone who'd obey orders, and start fighting back. Here he was as useless as a kitten, while his people and his dream were being smashed.

Suddenly white smoke began gushing from the rocket tubes. Detcharn screamed incoherently. They were blowing up the rockets! Another explosion from overhead slammed him hard against the railing.

Something struck him hard from behind. His head and chest went clear over the railing. He clawed frantically at empty air, and only succeeded in destroying what was left of his balance. For a moment he hung upside down, his toes hooked over the railing. The moment was long enough for him to see Arsha standing there, naked but with a triumphant grin on her face.

Then as he reached for her ankles, she smashed her fists down on Detcharn's feet. His last hold on the railing broke, and he plummeted down into space. He had enough time to scream out one last desperate denial that this could be happening to him, before he struck the outward slope of the cliff. Then only a senseless, bloody doll was left to finish its three-hundred foot fall.

*   *   *

184

Shangbari was enjoying himself. After all, what better game for a great hunter than Doimari? There was both honor and vengeance in killing them—more honor, because of the vengeance.

He still did not let himself get so busy killing that he forgot to count the explosions that his men set off. Voros had said plainly, "All the fire-beams on the top of the cliff must die. Otherwise they will destroy our sky-machines. Then we will not be able to fly away, and kill more Doimari some other time."

Shangbari did not fear dying, but he did want to kill many more Doimari before he did. He also wanted to please Voros so that he would lead the Red Cats against the Doimari again. So he was very careful in counting the explosions as his men smashed the fire-beams.

The woman warrior Sparra walked beside him. She also seemed to be enjoying herself. Such pleasure in killing was strange in a woman, but then Shangbari reminded himself that Sparra was as much warrior as woman.

They came to what seemed to be a small door set in the ground. Sparra motioned that Shangbari should stand back, then pulled one of the small hand-bombs out of her pouch. She was about to throw it when the door opened and five Doimari ran out shooting. One of them hit Sparra as the bomb left her hand. She fell, and the explosion of the bomb knocked her over the edge of the cliff. She did not cry out, so Shangbari knew she must be senseless or dead.

Fortunately the bomb killed or wounded the five Doimari. Shangbari finished off the wounded ones with his knife, then looked over the edge of the cliff. He was surprised to see that Sparra had not fallen far. She lay in a sort of nest of wires hung on poles sticking out of the cliff—an "antenna," Voros had called it. If she was still alive Shangbari knew he had to get her back. And even if she was dead—well, Voros had told them not to try bringing home bodies, but would he say that about his own woman?

Shangbari found that he could not reach Sparra's ankles with his arms at full stretch. To get a good grip, he needed help himself. So he called to four men to hold him, two on each leg, and let him down until he could grab Sparra. Then the four pulled both Shangbari and Sparra back up over the edge of the cliff. She was alive when they laid her down, because her eyes flickered. Then a great gush of blood came out of her mouth and she went limp.

As Shangbari knelt to close her eyes, the long-awaited seventh explosion went off. He saw the last fire-beam machine fly out into the air in pieces. That was good to see, but he did not like what he saw after that. A great slab of the face of the cliff fell after the machine, then smaller pieces. Cracks elsewhere showed that before long more of the cliff might fall away.

Shangbari liked even less what he felt under his feet. The ground went on shaking even after the explosion, as if someone were hitting the cliff face with a gigantic hammer. The others kneeling beside Sparra felt it, too. He did not have to urge them twice to pick her up and move away from the edge of the cliff.

Some of the others were doubtful. "Even if the demons in the rock are waking, what of it?" one said. "We have destroyed the last fire-beam. Surely they will go back to sleep now that we no longer set off bombs in their ears?"

In reply Shangbari pointed at the base on the level ground below. It was almost completely hidden in smoke by now, but new spurts of flame shot up every minute or so. "*They* will not let the demons sleep, and indeed why should they? Their work is not done. Ours is. Let us return to the sky-machine, so that it may swiftly carry us away from the demons if they come out to attack us."

He had to threaten a couple of sluggish fools with duels, to take place after they returned to the village.

186

And if Ikhnan objected, then let him object! In the end everybody followed Shangbari back to the sky-machines.

When the explosions kept going off after the surviving Tribesmen got back to the guardhouse, Blade started worrying. The fires must be traveling through the underground fuel pipes. That was fine, up to a point. But what if the fires reached the main fuel dump and set it off prematurely?

Blade didn't know how much fuel the main dump held, or what kind. He was pretty sure it was a lot, and potent. If it all went off at once—but that was why he'd time the charges at the dump to go off *after* the raiders were airborne again.

He looked around at his raiders. Everyone who was going to get back was back—twenty-eight of the forty in the two lifters here, some of the wounded. "Get everybody into the second lifter," he told Ezarn and Ikhnan. "I'll take the one with the laser turret."

"It's going to be tight," said Ezarn.

"No worse than it was coming out, with twenty people and the explosives," said Blade. "With the second lifter flying light, I can maneuver it more easily. That could be important, if there's anybody left around here with some fight in him."

Loaded to capacity, the first lifter took off. As Blade, Cheeky, and Ezarn got into the second, they saw the third lifter heading toward them from the top of the cliff. Then Blade was too busy getting his lifter airborne, while Ezarn strapped down a heavy Doimari laser he'd acquired somewhere.

Once they were in the air, Blade breathed easier. He'd been afraid to the last moment that something would break one of the germ cylinders. Unless Kaldak's scientists had been able to turn the formula into a usable serum, that could mean a horrible death for—

It was like the sun coming up from deep inside the earth. A monstrous ball of orange fire rose where the main fuel dump had been, carrying with it slabs of concrete, clods of earth, and parts of buildings weighing many tons. With deceptive slowness, the fireball swelled, swallowing everything in its path. The shock wave reached the guardhouse and tore it apart, but before the pieces could go far the flames caught up with them.

Then the shockwave hit the lifter, tossing it like a leaf in a gale. Blade was even busier than before, and not quite sure he was going to be able to stay in the air at all. Ezarn clung to anything which offered a handhold, and cursed the Doimari, lifters, air travel, rockets, and his own folly in letting himself be talked into coming along on this raid.

At last the air quieted down and the smoke cleared away enough to give Blade a good look at the damage. Where the main fuel dump had been was a smoking crater. Around it for a mile in all directions lay blackened wreckage. The base couldn't have been much more thoroughly wrecked with an atomic bomb.

"We could have done the whole damned job with that," said Ezarn. Looking over Blade's shoulder. "Saved a lot of good men, too." He seemed to be expecting Blade to say something, then added, "Well, I don't care *what* shape the Tribesmen's ears were. They were damned good. *Damned* good." He muttered that several more times as he went back to the laser turret and started strapping himself in.

Blade grinned, at more than Ezarn's newfound tolerance. They could stop worrying about the fever germs now. The blast must have fractured every cylinder—but the wall of flame on its heels must have sterilized their contents as completely as a bacteriologist could have asked for. There would be no fever let loose on this Dimension, even by accident.

The three lifters met over what was left of the main blockhouse. With propellers throttled back so that they hung in the sky, the men in them could talk back and forth without radio. Blade didn't want any Doimari eavesdropping.

"Sparra is dead, Voros," said Shangbari. "We brought away her body, so that she might lie among her own people."

Blade swallowed. Sparra dead. He would—think about it later. At least she'd been a volunteer who died with a gun in her hand, not an innocent victim of somebody else's madness, like Moshra.

"Does anyone know what happened to the Seeker Detcharn?" he asked. No one seemed to. Blade was about to give orders for the course home, when a sudden rumble and roar drowned out the whine of the propellers. Everyone looked around wildly, fearing some unknown form of attack—then stopped to stare at the cliff.

Slowly but steadily, the whole cliff which held the laboratory complex was collapsing. Pieces of stone the size of Seekers' mansions were sliding down or falling freely, landing on top of other pieces, throwing up explosions of dust and gravel. Blade saw flashes of sunlight on metal, as laboratory equipment, steel beams, and elevator shafts tore loose and fell with the stone. Blade thought he saw human figures also falling, arms and legs flailing wildly.

There must have been a geological fault in the cliff, which had finally fractured under the hammering from the explosions. It was a more thorough destruction of the Seekers than Blade had planned or even wanted, but now it didn't matter if Detcharn were dead or not. Most of the Seekers and their laboratories were gone, their power in Doimar was smashed, and their city's technology would surely fall behind Kaldak's.

Considering how the stones were flying, it was time to get out of here. Also, by now the Doimari in their main city must have learned of the attack on the rocket base, and would have sent out lifters to apprehend the raiders. "Follow me," said Blade. "We're heading straight for the city of Doimar." They all stared and he explained. "That's the last direction they'll expect us to go. By the time we get to the city,

189

all the lifters will be on their way out here or to the border. Then we'll go to ground beyond Doimar and cross the border at night."

They obviously thought he was crazy, but then he was Voros the Wise, who'd led them to victory and vengeance over the Doimari. Also, if they thought he was crazy, the Doimari would probably think the same.

Blade hoped he was guessing right. He also hoped that Feragga wouldn't take a hand in guiding the search for the raiders. She just might; now that Blade had carried out her plans for stopping Detcharn. After all, Blade *was* primarily helping the Kaldakans, her age-old enemies, and even though Feragga said she wanted peace, she certainly wouldn't hesitate to apprehend the raiders in order to make examples of them. This would be just like Feragga, and it could just mean the end to Blade, for she was the one person in Doimar who knew how his mind really worked.

Chapter 25

Baliza was walking along a sandy beach by the ocean. She'd never seen the ocean, but somehow she knew that the blue water stretching to the horizon was just that. A powerfully built man was walking beside her. He looked somewhat like Voros, but she knew that this was her father, the Sky Master Blade.

Either he was a giant, or she'd shrunk. She'd just realized that neither was the case, that she was a little girl again, when she heard the waves starting to whisper her name.

"Baliza, Baliza."

"Go away."

"Baliza!" This was no wave, but a human voice. She turned to ask her father what to do, but he was no longer there. Then the beach and the ocean faded away, and she felt the blankets of her bed in Doimar over her. Someone was shaking her.

"Baliza?"

It was Kandro. "What is it?" she muttered, still half-asleep and more than half-angry at being awakened from a dream she thought might have answered so many questions.

"Something's happened. Something big. I think there's been an army mutiny. Soldiers are all over the place."

"Lifters, too?"

"Yes. Whole balloon trains, too, heading for the border."

Baliza snapped wide-awake in a moment. She also cursed under her breath. It would be just her luck, to have Voros—she still could not call him "her father" —stage his raid on the rocket base *now*. She couldn't think of anything else which could be causing this kind of uproar and troop movements.

She would have a few words for her stepfather, Sidas, when she got back to Kaldak—*if* she got back. He'd refused to time her carrying off Feragga with the raid. He'd said that would endanger the secrecy of both projects. He'd even refused to let her inform the three Intelligence people who were helping her in Doimar. Again, the excuse was secrecy. What they didn't know, they couldn't be tortured into telling.

She'd swallowed it then, because she'd had no choice. Now, getting to Feragga would be a lot more difficult. Everyone would be on the alert, and the two agents who were supposed to steal a lifter might run into trouble. Even Feragga's two guards might be suspicious enough to put up a fight.

On the other hand, it was now all the more important to try for Feragga. Her enemies might take advantage of the confusion to try killing her. Baliza knew the old woman deserved a better fate than being shot down by the hired killers of a slimy madman like Detcharn.

She sprang out of bed, and Kandro blinked. She'd forgotten that she was sleeping naked. She giggled. She'd really have to go to bed with the poor little fellow, so he'd get used to her skin. But why did the idea of any man in her bed except Monitor Bekror suddenly seem odd, almost unpleasant?

Time to worry about that later. She pulled on her clothes every which way, then reluctantly tidied them. The neighborhood where her inn lay was rather poor and shabby, but Feragga lived in a richer quarter. She and Kandro shouldn't look as if they had spent the night sleeping in the streets.

When she knew her clothes were in order and her weapons were concealed, she threw a final look around the room to see if she'd left any clues behind. She saw none, and led Kandro down the stairs two at a time.

Feragga's building was too far for them to run all the way, as much as Baliza was tempted to do so. She fought down the urge. They'd get there exhausted, even if they didn't attract too much notice on the way. So they walked briskly, and Baliza watched the sky overhead and the streets around them on the way.

Certainly Voros's raid or something just as big must have happened. Every soldier she saw was moving as fast as she was, and most ordinary Doimari were staying inside or at least out of the soldiers' way. Lifters were also going overhead in swarms. Even though Baliza knew that Doimar had more lifters than Kaldak, she still hadn't expected to see so many. She thanked the Laws that she'd ordered the two lifter-thieves to steal a citizen's machine. All the soldiers' lifters would now be closely guarded.

They reached the street of Feragga's building, and Kandro grabbed her arm. "Look. Our people must be there already." A lifter was just settling down on Feragga's roof.

Baliza squinted into the sun, then shook her head. "Not unless they got away with a soldiers' lifter. That one's got army markings on it. Come on!" They had to be in the building and out of sight from the roof before the soldiers in that lifter started getting out. After that—well, she would see. This wasn't a "Do it or don't come back alive" mission—Sidas didn't give that kind of orders. But she had her pride in doing the impossible and making it look easy. Sidas said that was another thing she seemed to have got from her father.

They charged into the building and headed up the stairs. Three flights up, and one to go, they heard the ominous crackle of lasers. At the foot of the last flight of stairs they heard a scream. It sounded like a

193

man's scream, thank the Lords! Then two bodies crashed down the stairs, locked together in a death-grapple. One was a Doimari soldier, the other, one of Feragga's guards.

The two Kaldakans looked at each other, then up the stairs. Things *seemed* clear. Baliza wished briefly for a grenade, then decided she wouldn't have dared throw it, not without knowing where Feragga was.

Lasers crackled again as they ran up the stairs. Baliza was the first to reach the top floor. As she stepped into the open two soldiers stepped out of a door across the hall. She shot one and he fell against his comrade, spoiling the man's aim. Before he could shoot again, Baliza kicked him in the stomach, then smashed him across the back of the neck with both hands as he doubled up.

From where she stood, Baliza now had a clear view down the hall to the open roof and the door of the lifter. The hall was smoke-filled and smelled of burned human flesh, but the lifter's pilot also had a clear view of her. He fired a solid-shot at her, and succeeded in hitting Kandro as he stepped out into the hall.

Kandro shot back as he fell. He'd won prizes for pistol shooting, and now proved the prizes had gone to the right man. The pilot flew out of his chair, headless. Baliza shot the man who tried to pull him away from the controls.

That seemed to be the last soldier. Baliza was trying to think what she'd do if there were any more, when she heard wheels on the rug behind her. Then:

"Put your hands up and turn around—slowly."

It was a strong voice, but with a note of old age. Baliza obeyed. She wasn't surprised to find herself looking at Feragga. The older woman was in her wheelchair, with one hand on its controls and the other holding a short, thick-barreled laser rifle.

Recognition was mutual. Feragga's eyes widened. "What in the name of everything unLawful—! Baliza! What are you doing in Doimar?"

194

Baliza didn't lower her hands but snapped out her reply. "To get you out of the city. And I don't think I've come a day too soon!"

Feragga looked up and down the hall, counting the bodies as if she was seeing them for the first time. Then she nodded. "No, I don't suppose you have. All right. I'll go."

Baliza's jaw dropped. Even though every second counted, she'd still expected to spend some time arguing. She almost suspected a trick or a trap. Why should Feragga be so tame and ready to flee to her city's hereditary enemies?

Yet if Feragga was telling the truth, this was a gift of minutes which might save them all. Baliza decided not to question the gift. She knelt beside Kandro, who was unconscious and pale from loss of blood but still breathing.

Feragga looked on approvingly as Baliza bandaged her companion's wounds. "Your father would have done that," she said. "He never abandoned friends. Your mother owes her life to that."

"I know."

"Nungor, my old war captain, was like that, too. It was a sad and un-Lawful thing, that he and Blade could not have met in a way that let them be friends. But life is that way, more often than not."

Baliza had no attention to spare for life's tragedies. Instead, she hoisted Kandro over her shoulder and carried him out to the lifter. Then she returned for Feragga. The old woman's grip on her rifle was so loose that Baliza was tempted to grab it. She resisted the idea. Feragga obviously wasn't going to be taken alive, and in fact it was this determination which had kept her fighting long enough for Baliza and Kandro to arrive. Snatching her rifle would just make her angry, without helping a bit against other Doimari.

Baliza wheeled Feragga, rifle and all, down the hall and into the lifter. She was strapping the chair firmly in place when she heard lifter propellers and the crackle of laser fire outside. They seemed to be a long way off but getting rapidly closer.

Baliza looked out. A battered and dirty citizen's lifter was heading for them. A hundred yards behind was a Doimari soldiers' machine, with men firing lasers from both doors and windows. They'd already hit the lifter in front several times, but the propellers were still intact.

A moment later Baliza recognized the other two Intelligence people in the pilots' seats. A moment after that, a shot from their pursuers got home. One propeller disintegrated. Baliza saw one of the Intelligence men throw up his hands as flying metal drove into him.

"Here, girl. It's heavier." Baliza turned at the words and took Feragga's rifle. It wouldn't do much good soon enough, but at least she owed it to the men and her own conscience to go down—

Her finger was on the trigger when the captured lifter suddenly swung around in a sharp turn. The turn took it directly into the path of the Doimari lifter. The captured lifter was moving slowly, but the Doimari lifter was speeding up as its pilot closed in for the kill. The impact as the two machines came together was enough to wreck both.

They bounced apart, spewing pieces and smoke, then began their long fall to the ground. Baliza didn't take her eyes off them until they both plunged through the roof of a building three streets away. Smoke boiled up, and she imagined she heard screams.

"Come on, girl," said Feragga irritably. "You can't do anything for them. It's wasting their deaths not to use the time they gave you! It's Detcharn's men who were coming for me. If what's happening is what I thought might happen, he'll be too busy to send more until we're—"

Baliza cursed, then glared at Feragga. "Old woman, just exactly what *did* you think might happen? And I
196

want an answer, or we don't move an inch off this roof!"

Faragga grinned. "That would really be cutting off your toes to spite your feet, now wouldn't it? But indeed, you ought to know. I suspect you'll be finding out from someone else before long, but—" She broke off, as Baliza let out a gasp as if she'd been punched in the stomach. Somehow she knew what had to be coming.

"It's time you knew. Your father the Sky Master Blade has come back. He's probably stamping Detcharn and the rocket base into the ground right now."

"My fa—ther?" It was a croak. She'd known it, but still she couldn't face hearing "Your father's come back" said like "The sun will rise tomorrow."

"You probably know him as Voros," Feragga went on. "But it's Blade all right. His Doimari daughter Moshra got it out of his mind. There's no doubt about it. "I—Lord's sake girl, what's gotten into you?"

Baliza shook herself like a wet dog. "Sorry. It's—going to take a little—for me to get used to it."

"Then do it elsewhere. Right now, you stop standing there like you're seeing your first naked man, and get this sky-barge moving. Otherwise your father's going to get a message about your glorious death, and a fine welcome-home present *that'll* be for him!"

Baliza said nothing, but she was at the controls in a moment. In another minute, the lifter was climbing swiftly into a temporarily empty sky.

Chapter 26

Far off on the horizon, Blade saw the towers of the city of Doimar. The sight actually made him breathe easier. They were now as close to the enemy's heart as they were going to get. They still hadn't met opposition or even suspicion.

Blade would have breathed still easier if there hadn't been quite so many lifters in the air. So far none of them were asking awkward questions, but if somebody did get suspicious, he could quickly call up strong reinforcements.

However, the Doimari would hardly sit quiet and twiddle their thumbs in the face of the raiders' victory. It was inevitable that they would be rushing around both on the ground and in the air, like ants from a kicked anthill. As long as they weren't any better organized, Blade thought he and his people had a reasonably good chance of getting out. They'd done their work, no matter what happened now, but Blade didn't like unnecessary kamikaze missions.

Ezarn had finished checking out the turret laser and pronounced it "tight and ready." Now he sat cross-legged beside Cheeky, doing the same check on his captured Doimari laser. With both side doors open, Ezarn could fire out either one, and the laser was powerful enough to hurt a lifter.

Doimar and the bee-swarm of lifters over it sank below the horizon. The raiders were alone over countryside that was mostly farms, with patches of forest.

Slowly the patches of forest grew larger, then grew together. In another few hours they would be outside the area which Doimar tried to control. They could go to ground in a forest which would hide them like a haystack hiding a needle, and wait until the hunt died down. Then they could swing far to the south and head for home. It would not be too different from the route Blade had used in escaping from Doimar with Kareena, except that they would be flying instead of using a hovercraft.

"Voros," said Ezarn quietly. "We're being followed."

Blade shifted position so that he could see out one of the side doors. Ezarn was right. A Doimari military lifter was overhauling them quickly. From its nose jutted the muzzle of a heavy laser. In a fixed mount, it wouldn't be as easy to aim as the one in Blade's turret, but it would be much more powerful. It could knock one of the raiders' lifters out of the sky with a single hit, or at least kill everyone aboard it.

Baliza had just discovered the big laser mounted in the nose of her lifter when she saw the three other machines a mile ahead. She mentally kicked herself for not having done a more thorough inspection of her prize long before this. Here she was facing Doimari she almost certainly would have to fight or outrun, and she hadn't even checked out her main weapon!

She was starting that overdue check when she saw something familiar about one of the lifters ahead. It had a turret-mounted laser forward—just like one of the machines sent to Voros. And all three lifters were smoke-blackened and scarred, as if they'd recently been in a fight—or near an explosion. . . .

Baliza fed power to the propellers and put the nose of her lifter down. With gravity aiding thrust, she rapidly caught up with the three machines and slid under them. Down here the turret of the landing machine couldn't bear on her, and nobody could lean out far enough to shoot without risking a fall.

"What Law-forsaken rat's in your brain, girl—?" began Feragga. Then Baliza pulled her machine up to fly parallel to the leader and only a few yards away.

"Well, I'll be buggered with a file," said Feragga softly. "Fine place for a family reunion this is, I must say." They both recognized the Sky Master Blade at the controls of the turreted lifter. For a moment which seemed to go on for hours, father and daughter stared at each other through the windows and across the empty air.

Then Blade seemed to shrug, smiled, and raised one hand in an open-palmed signal of greeting.

When Blade saw his daughter at the controls of the lifter alongside, and Feragga strapped in her wheelchair, his breath went out with a *whoooosh*. The secret of his identity and probably the Dimension X secret were so far up the spout they'd probably never get back down again. The idea of Feragga not telling Baliza the truth about "Voros" was too ridiculous to contemplate.

So that question was settled. But—what were Baliza and Feragga doing out here in the same lifter? Was his daughter kidnapping Feragga or rescuing her? Rescuing, probably—Blade now saw the hefty laser in Feragga's lap. And her grin as she recognized him didn't look like a prisoner's, either.

Time to settle that question when they'd landed and he and the others could get off and talk quietly. He'd be damned if he was going to reveal his identity over the radio hundreds of miles inside Doimar! The secret was out, but maybe he could still keep it from getting too far out.

He signaled that Baliza should take position at the rear of the line. She nodded, and her machine started dropping back. As it did, Blade saw Ezarn staring hard at him.

"Voros, that was Baliza, wasn't it?"

"Unless she's got a twin, yes."

"And the other woman, the old one. That was Feragga, wasn't it?"

"As far as I can tell, yes."

"Wonder how far that is, Voros. Wonder if you *are* really a—*Voros*, in fact."

Ezarn wouldn't do anything violent or dangerous even if he wasn't told the truth. But he'd been too good a soldier and too loyal a friend to be told anything else. He deserved the truth more than anybody in this Dimension except the young woman who'd already found it out.

"I am—" he began then Ezarn shouted:

"Look out!"

A laser beam ripped past. It came from below and off to the right. As Ezarn sprang into the turret, Blade spotted the Doimari lifter rising from behind a clump of tall trees in the forest below.

So did Ezarn. The turret lazer went *tsssrrpppp!* and a piece of the other lifter's hull glowed, then peeled away. It slammed against the trees, but its own laser was also turret-mounted. In spite of the unstable platform under him, the turret gunner shot back. Smoke, hot air, and bits of molten metal sprayed back at Ezarn as the enemy beam took off the barrel of his laser.

Ezarn fell back into the cabin, coughing, cursing, and beating out burning spots on his clothes. He was making so much noise that Blade was fairly sure he wasn't badly hurt. Cheeky squalled in rage and alarm but had the sense to stay out from underfoot.

Then Blade saw two more lifters rising from the bank of a small river. He didn't know if the detachment's commander was trigger-happy or if he'd been warned somehow. If he was attacking on his own initiative and his detachment was wiped out, the raiders might still escape.

Not if Blade used his radio, though. He'd just have to trust to Baliza's good sense, to make her pick sound tactics. "Ezarn, get your own laser and stand ready by the doors. I'm going down under them."

"Right, Voros!" Ezarn scrambled into position so fast that Blade stopped worrying about his being hurt. He concentrated on the controls, putting the lifter into a dive with the propellers wide open.

He'd covered half the distance to the enemy before they saw him coming.

The attack was a complete surprise to Baliza. Before she'd recovered from the surprise, the first enemy lifter had plunged to the ground and exploded. Then she saw her father's lifter plunging straight at the other two enemies.

"May the Laws protect us," she breathed. She saw again the sight of the two Intelligence men, ramming the enemy at the cost of their own lives. She imagined her father falling down through the sky in a smashed lifter, his body crushed and charred but still horribly alive after it struck. She heard his screams—then let out one of her own.

"No!"

The Doimari would have both her and her father or neither of them.

She put her lifter's nose down and fed it power. At the same time, she was adjusting the controls on the main laser. Its power supply was fully charged.

She swept past the other two lifters, ignoring the staring faces at their doors and window. Out in front, she saw that the enemy was reacting to her father's attack. But would they react fast enough, and how? If they didn't break to the right and left, he *would* ram them. But if they did break, where would they go? She estimated distances and times, made a careful adjustment of her own lifter's course, then rested one finger on the firing button.

The two Doimari lifters broke, one hard to the right, the other hard to the left. A laser beam darted out of Blade's door at the one on the right. The one on the left swung out wide, precisely on the course Baliza had predicted. She stabbed the firing button.

Laser beam and lifter met in a perfect mating.

She must have hit the power supply, because the enemy lifter blew apart like a hand grenade. White-hot pieces arched down through the sky from a cloud of sparks and blue smoke.

The other lifter and Blade's were now too close together to let Baliza risk a second shot. She clenched her gun hand into a fist to keep her finger off the button.

Another blazing exchange of laser beams. Blade's machine was hit, and hard—it started to lurch down-ward toward the river. If it lost all lift this high—Baliza forced the thought out of her mind.

Then she saw that the last enemy lifter was wandering aimlessly in circles, its nose smoking, its pilot apparently dead or hurt. It showed no signs of falling.

It showed no signs of maneuvering, either, as Baliza got into position behind and lasered it. This one didn't explode, but it was a lifeless, smoking wreck as it plunged into the river in a cloud of steam.

The waves from the crash were still spreading when Blade's lifter made a slightly more dignified landing in the river. It promptly started to sink, but Baliza sighed with relief when she saw her father and another man climb out on the roof. There was also something small and blue riding on her father's shoulder.

She started down toward the river, while the other two raider lifters flew in circles above her.

The last air was bubbling out of the sinking lifter when Blade saw his daughter waving to him out of her cockpit window. She cut the propellers back and came to a stop almost overhead.

"You first, Ezarn," he said. "Then I'll hand up Cheeky."

Ezarn tossed the laser up into the open door and swung himself up. He was leaning over the edge to

203

reach for Cheeky when the feather-monkey leaped. He sailed clear over Ezarn and vanished into the lifter. By then the water was up to Blades's knees. Baliza lowered her lifter another foot, and Ezarn yanked him in so hard Blade felt his arms and shoulders protesting. It was still better than an impromptu swim in a river which might hold anything, most of it mutated and all of it hungry.

As the lifter rose, Blade went forward. He looked carefully at the wounded Intelligence man lying on the floor of the cabin; he appeared to be safely unconscious. Each step seemed longer to Blade than the last, and the final step up to his daughter in the pilot's seat seemed the longest of all. Then Blade consigned the Dimension X secret to the devil, bent down, and kissed Baliza on the forehead.

"You're a daughter to be proud of," was all he felt able to say. He was afraid his voice wouldn't stay steady for more than that.

"Sidas was afraid of you worrying about *my* safety," said Baliza softly. "He didn't think I might find a time to be worried about—yours." She raised one hand and wiped the back of it across her eyes. "Father . . ."

"What's the matter, girl?" said Feragga with a chuckle. "That wasn't the way you greeted him the last time you met, I've heard."

"Oh, shut up, you bawdy old witch," growled Blade. "Or better yet, make yourself useful. Get on the *radio*—the Sky Voice—and listen to the talk between the Doimari lifters. That may tell us if anyone heard a call from the ones we shot down."

"Yes, Sky Master," said Feragga with sarcastic meekness.

Blade grinned. He understood now what Feragga had been doing—trying to keep him and Baliza from being completely carried away by their emotions. She'd probably been right, too. This far inside Doimari territory, they were a long way from being out of the woods yet.

204

*   *   *

Feragga listened for an hour without hearing any signs that the battle by the river had been detected. Apparently the Doimari commander had been acting on his own initiative and sent out no messages before he went down.

By then it was mid-afternoon. Blade started searching for a clearing where he could land and hide the lifters. He wanted to find it, get the lifters out of sight, and make camp before dark.

Chapter 27

Ikhnan himself and Shangbari were the only two of the Red Cats to go with Voros at dawn to the sky-machines which would take him to the City of Kaldak. The rest of the Tribe, warriors and women alike, were too drunk or sound asleep.

Not that Shangbari would have called himself sober. There had been much beer drunk last night, and even some strong Kaldakan waters from Monitor Bekror's house. All wanted to celebrate the victory and the escape and give the spirits of the dead a proper start toward the Great Hunt. Voros the Wise drank as much as anyone, for he had won the victory but had his woman Sparra to mourn.

And the cunning of the escape! That was worth much beer all by itself. Flying so far into Doimar that no map showed where they were, then sitting in the forest for days while the Doimari looked for them in all the places they were not. Shangbari had fed them well during those days with his hunting skills, although some of the animals were strange even to him. He was as proud of how well they'd eaten because of his skills as he was of the Doimari he'd killed at the wizards' home.

No one would ever again doubt that Shangbari was the finest hunter of the Red Cats. And Shangbari knew he owed this also to Voros the Wise, a man of the City of Kaldak.

Clearly the gods had made many kinds of City men—and women.

Now Voros and Ezarn stood beside their machine, waiting for the chief and the hunter to come up. Cheeky and the Red Cat Fija were sitting face to face at their feet, like two human friends saying farewell.

"Farewell, Ikhnan, Shangbari," said Voros. "If it is so willed, I shall return to do you more honor."

"The greatest honor you can do is leading us again in battle, if there is a worthy enemy to be fought," said Ikhnan. Shangbari nodded.

"That would be a pleasure, if it can be so," said Voros. "I have never led better fighting men than the Red Cats."

"I've never fought beside better, neither," said Ezarn, although he looked at the ground as he said it instead of at the two Tribesmen.

Then Voros's face set hard. Cheeky jumped up on his shoulder, and he and Ezarn climbed into the sky machine. It rose, and the other three rose with it. Like birds flying away for the winter, they vanished over the treetops.

Shangbari looked at Ikhnan. "I wonder why Voros looks as if he was going to punishment instead of honor for his victory?"

"Perhaps he has offended someone powerful in Kaldak," said the chief. "There have always been those in the Cities who wanted them to unite against the Tribes, not fight each other. Certainly they would not be happy that he has won his victory with our aid!"

Ikhnan was shrewd, as usual. "They will find him hard to kill," said Shangbari. "Ezarn will guard his back to the death, and so will Baliza."

Shangbari did not know what to make of the woman Baliza, other than that she seemed to be a warrior-woman even more formidable than Sparra. Sometimes she behaved as if she had once been Voros's woman. Other times she behaved as if she was blood kin, unlawful for him to bed. Well, either way she would be sworn to defend or avenge him.

*   *   *

Short of a firing squad, Blade wasn't really sure what to expect on his return to Kaldak. He'd finally stopped worrying about the Dimension X secret to the point where he could see things from the point of view of the Kaldakans. After all, his return from the dead must have thrown a rather large wrench in *their* works, too!

So it was pleasant but not completely a surprise to discover what Sidas planned to do about the Sky Master's return. Once he'd listened to Blade's story, he thanked Blade, poured out beer, and said:

"We're not going to tell anybody a damned thing. Not a word. As far as we're concerned, the raid was led by Cadet Commander Voros, who's going to get a pardon and a company of his own."

The High Commander laughed. "This is partly because we respect you and the way you wanted to keep your return a secret. But don't flatter yourself that's the only reason."

"That's no way to talk to—" began Baliza, but Sidas waved her to silence.

"It's the way to talk to a soldier of Kaldak. I want to think of Blade that way, if I can. And that's another reason why I don't want the news to get out. Consider how few people will even try to think of the Sky Master as just another man. Consider how many are going to think of him as a god who came to get us out of trouble again. If too many of them think that, they'll be expecting him to come back and save them *every* time Kaldak gets into trouble.

"Also, from what Blade says, it will be a century or more before we can use his method of traveling between the—*Dimensions?*" Blade nodded. Sidas went on. "A century, before the 'brains' we use in our Fighting Machines are good enough. But people won't believe that. They'll expect a miracle tomorrow, ask our scientists to produce it, then tear them apart if they don't."

Blade nodded again. He wasn't entirely sure it

would take a whole century for Kaldak to develop the computers. They might even find some other method of inter-Dimensional travel. Such existed, and there just weren't that many rules on the subject.

However, Sidas's mistake wouldn't do anyone any harm. If someone in this Dimension did get inter-Dimensional travel, it was more likely to be Doimar, with its Seekers and telepaths. The raid had undoubtedly set them back a couple of generations, but it hadn't completely wiped out their City's advantage.

"Yes," said Baliza "We've got better things to do than hunt the Golden Munfan. Also, if no one knows that Blade saved us again, nobody will say anything against the High Command or the Intelligence people."

"What's there to say against me?" said Sidas.

"A lot, when my father's not around to tell me I should be more respectful to a superior," said Baliza.

Sidas grunted. "All right."

Blade smiled. He was pretty sure what Baliza had to say and could almost feel sorry for Sidas. Baliza still wasn't happy about the lack of coordination between her mission and Blade's, even though everybody had been lucky. She was going to have some things to say about desk-bound superiors. They would probably be the same things *he'd* said in his younger days, when he'd felt he was carrying the can for their mistakes.

That evening Sidas threw a party, for everyone who was in on the secret.

It was a highly informal party, with nobody standing on rank. Even Ezarn finally got used to talking to Monitor Bekror and taking a glass of beer from a tray held by his High Commander. He still looked a bit as if he'd been hit over the head and hadn't quite recovered. Blade expected the man would sooner or later get used to the fact that his old comrade Voros was really the Sky Master Blade. Ezarn wasn't stupid, he was impossible to frighten, and having an assured

209

future (in the Monitor Bekror's guards, with a farm of his own) probably wouldn't hurt either.

Cheeky ate so much that finally he vomited all over Baliza's tunic. She washed him off, put him to bed, then went around the rest of the evening bare to the waist. For the first time in his life Blade found himself trying *not* to look at such a good-looking woman parading around half-bare. However, he finally remembered that this was Kaldakan custom. Blood kin had a complete right to be casually nude around each other.

"It's good to see her that way," Bekror told Blade as they both refilled their cups. "I wouldn't care to have some unnatural fear crawling in her mind when I marry her."

Blade looked at his cup, to see if somebody had spiked his drink. Or maybe he'd just drunk too much?

"I thought you said you wanted to marry Baliza," he said slowly.

"I did," said Bekror. "If she'll have me."

"And if she won't?"

"She's the best woman I've known for a long time. She's not the only one. If she says no, I'll let her go. I value my peace of mind too much."

"Not to mention your ribs, skull, and back teeth," added Blade.

"Them, too."

They talked freely after that. Bekror wanted a wife who would outlive him and be able to take care of his estates and any children she had by him.

"About the taking care, I'm not worried," said Blade. "About the outliving—well, she's got one of my worst habits. She'll always run to find out what's happening, no matter how dangerous it might be."

"She'll have a double dose of it, then. Her mother was like that." They both drank to Kareena's memory. "What do you suggest my doing about it?"

"Learn to live with it, or you'll have to learn to live without her," said Blade flatly.

"That's all?"

210

"That's all. And you didn't really need my advice, did you?"

Blade wanted out of this embarrassing situation of advising a prospective son-in-law who was almost old enough to be his own father, about a daughter whom the other man surely knew much better than he did! Inter-Dimensional family reunions were a headache.

Blade, Feragga, and Baliza left the party by midnight, while they were all still sober enough to fly. They were going south, to meet the one man Blade wanted to see who hadn't been at the party. It would have caused too much talk, to recall Bairam from his exile in the south.

Feragga was going south with them, to wait out the crisis in Doimar. "I'm going back as soon as I'm sure I'll be heard instead of shot at," she said bluntly. "And if that doesn't happen—if I have to stay in Kaldak—I'm not going to ask anyone to come. Anybody who wants to come to me from Doimar, that's up to them."

"We risked—" Baliza began, but her father put a hand on her shoulder.

"I know what you risked, and I know what you did. That destruction of the cliff—it wasn't your fault, but the Seekers died. *My* Seekers, more than Detcharn's.

"I'm grateful to be alive. I'm still not grateful enough to be a traitor, and there's nothing you can do to change my mind on that. Nor you either, Blade," she said with a grin. "I've still got a soft heart for you, but not a soft head."

Blade had the feeling that before long the Kaldakans were going to wish they'd left Feragga in Doimar! He couldn't completely share the feeling—he was too glad she was alive. But he wasn't at all surprised at her refusal to be a traitor. That was one more thing he could have told the Kaldakans in advance, if he hadn't been so carefully hiding his identity.

He made a mental note to talk with Feragga about

211

the use of rockets for space flight. If the Doimari got turned in that direction, it might keep them peaceful and would certainly help the whole Dimension recover. If only his son Detcharn had thought of that himself! His name might be honored in the history of this world, instead of cursed.

To their surprise, Geyrna met them at the lifter field. "Do you mind if I come along?" she said.

"Not if you don't mind telling me why," said Baliza.

"I want to talk to Feragga," Geyrna said. "The Koldak Council of Nine is going to ask why she won't jump through hoops for them. I'd like to have an answer for them. It may not save my seat, but it will save my conscience."

"How did you guess what I've just been telling these people?" demanded Feragga. "You aren't a mind-speaker, are you?"

Geyrna grinned sourly. "Just natural shrewdness—no, if I had that, I might still have a husband. And that's the other reason I'm going south. I want to try putting things back together with Bairam. He shouldn't have gone drinking the way he did, but—well, I did give him some reasons. Maybe they would have been reasons for any man, not just Bairam. I don't know. I want—" She squeezed her eyes shut as Baliza embraced her.

They would need two pilots for the flight south. Blade and Baliza tossed a coin for it, and Baliza won the first watch. As the lights of Kaldak faded behind them, Blade crawled aft and curled up on a pile of old parachutes. Cheeky curled up on his chest, one paw twined in Blade's beard. Blade couldn't remember when he'd last had a good night's sleep. While he was as tough as a diesel locomotive, he also knew the need to sleep when he could.

The worst *might* be over, but he refused to assume it was until he woke up back in Home Dimension.

Chapter 28

Something was wrong.

There was a blanket over Blade, and there hadn't been one in the lifter. Instead of the stiff parachutes, there was a cool sheet under him, smooth and with a smell that practically shouted, "Hospital!" Had the lifter crashed.

Perhaps. But Kaldak didn't have hospitals like that.

Blade opened his eyes, then sat up. He was in the familiar room in the Complex's private hospital where he spent a couple of days for observation after each trip. That was the rule, whether he came back wounded or not. The doctors wanted their piece out of him, and that was all there was to it!

He looked around the room. Hanging on the wall was the Kaldakan soldier's uniform he had worn on the flight to see Bairam in his place of exile in the south. Why the Complex's scientists hadn't yet absconded with it to conduct their experiments was a mystery, but then it was as hard now to believe what he was seeing as it had been to believe he was back in Kaldak. However, there was just as little point in ignoring what his senses were shouting to him.

He'd fallen asleep in Kaldak and awakened in Home Dimension. As simple as that—the simplest and easiest transition from one Dimension to another in the whole history of the Project!

And if that wasn't enough, this simple homecoming was the end of the most complicated, nerve-wracking mission in the history of the Project. Well, no. The fight against the Ngaa had been worse. But this return to Kaldak was certainly a bloody good second!

Blade laughed. Somewhere up above was a Higher Power with a taste for practical jokes. Whether you called him God, Buddha, Allah, or the Lord of the Laws, he had to exist. There was no other way to explain this sort of thing.

Then a thought made Blade's heart race so that the nurse on duty monitoring his vital signs nearly punched the emergency button.

Cheeky!

Yeeep? It sounded both sleepy and irritable, but it was close at hand. Blade reached for a light switch and searched the room again. There it was, in a corner—a large cage of heavy wire mesh coated with plastic, and Cheeky inside it.

They must have known he shouldn't be separated from Blade, but they couldn't quite bring themselves to let something as unsanitary as a feather-monkey loose in a hospital room. So they'd caged him.

The bastards and their rules! Blade punched the call button for the nurse and got out of bed, trailing wires. Cheeky was getting out of that cage *now*, and if the doctors fussed—well, he could always call up Lord Leighton. The scientist would be on his side, where Cheeky was concerned.

When the nurse arrived, Blade was sitting on the bed, scratching Cheeky behind the ears. He was smiling as he contemplated what Lord Leighton would say to the doctors if their stupidity got him dragged out of bed at night.

Blade stopped smiling when he contemplated what Leighton would say when he found out that people in Dimension X had learned about inter-Dimension travel. True, the technicians and scientists of Kaldak and Doimar were in no position at the moment to discover a method for traveling to other Dimensions, but in time—

Leighton wasn't going to be pleased, either, that

Blade and Cheeky had been separated upon arrival in Dimension X, and that Blade never found out anything about why he went to Kaldak and Cheeky went to Doimar. That might affect their plans for the next trip.

But at least Cheeky was here with him in Home Dimension. That and the fact that Blade had brought back with him the Kaldak uniform—made of a Oltec fabric and an Oltec kind of plastic—should certainly satisfy the scientist somewhat.

As for Blade, he was pleased enough that a balance of power now seemed to exist in the Dimension he had just visited. It had been necessary for the Doimari to lose some power and for the Tribes to gain some, but now, with Kaldak, they should all be able to live in a state of equilibrium and peace.

In a somewhat less well-equipped hospital in Doimar, the Seeker named Arsha propped herself up in bed. She was feeling much better today, and she knew it wouldn't be too much longer until she and her baby were discharged.

Arsha was the young scientist's assistant who had been experimenting on Cheeky at the research complex, before the feather-monkey had escaped and been reunited with Blade. She was also the one who had been punished by Detcharn but who had later seen to it that he fell to his death from the balcony railing. Arsha had also been one of the few Seekers to escape the cataclysm when the cliff had collapsed. During the chaos of the attack, she had managed to sneak down many flights of stairs, deep into the bowels of the earth, to the secret rooms where the baby Brant was kept. After the rocks and earth had settled, she had managed to carry the infant to safety through the long escape tunnel, which let out a mile away from the destroyed complex. Exhausted and badly shaken, she was spotted by a Doimari lifter and then taken to the City, where she claimed the baby was her own. Since all the other Seekers who

215

knew about the baby had died in the cataclysm, Arsha alone knew the infant's true identity: he was the son of *Du-Shro* Detcharn and his half-sister Moshra. He was thus the grandson of the Sky Master Blade.

She looked over to where the baby sat in his crib. He was watching her with his penetrating dark eyes, and he smiled and gurgled in delight when she turned to look at him. He certainly was a rugged-looking little boy, big for his age, with his sturdy body and black hair. He would grow up to be quite a man, perhaps even a god like the Sky Master himself.

BLADE

by Jeffrey Lord

More bestselling heroic fantasy from Pinnacle, America's #1 series publisher.
Over 3.5 million copies of Blade in print!

☐ 40-432-8 The Bronze Axe #1	$1.50
☐ 40-433-6 Jewel of Tharn #3	$1.50
☐ 41-721-7 Slave of Sarma #4	$2.25
☐ 40-435-2 Liberator of Jedd #5	$1.50
☐ 40-436-0 Monster of the Maze #6	$1.50
☐ 40-437-9 Pearl of Patmos #7	$1.50
☐ 40-438-7 Undying World #8	$1.50
☐ 40-439-5 Kingdom of Royth #9	$1.50
☐ 40-440-9 Ice Dragon #10	$1.50
☐ 40-441-7 King of Zunga #12	$1.75
☐ 40-787-4 Temples of Ayocan #14	$1.75
☐ 41-722-5 Towers of Melnon #15	$2.25
☐ 40-790-4 Mountains of Brega #17	$1.75

☐ 40-257-0 Champion of the Gods #21	$1.50
☐ 40-457-3 Forests of Gleor #22	$1.50
☐ 41-723-3 Empire of Blood #23	$2.25
☐ 40-260-0 Dragons of Englor #24	$1.50
☐ 40-444-1 Torian Pearls #25	$1.50
☐ 40-193-0 City of the Living Dead #26	$1.50
☐ 40-205-8 Master of the Hashomi #27	$1.50
☐ 40-206-6 Wizard of Rentoro #28	$1.50
☐ 40-207-4 Treasure of the Stars #29	$1.50
☐ 40-208-2 Dimension of Horror #30	$1.50
☐ 40-648-7 Gladiators of Hapanu #31	$1.50
☐ 41-724-1 Pirates of Gohar #32	$2.25
☐ 40-852-8 Killer Plants of Binaark #33	$1.75

Canadian orders must be paid with U.S. Bank check or U.S. Postal money order only.

Buy them at your local bookstore or use this handy coupon.

Clip and mail this page with your order

PINNACLE BOOKS, INC. — Reader Service Dept.
1430 Broadway, New York, NY 10018

Please send me the book(s) I have checked above. I am enclosing $_____ (please add 75¢ to cover postage and handling). Send check or money order only — no cash or C.O.D.'s.

Mr./Mrs./Miss _____

Address _____

City _____ State/Zip _____

Please allow six weeks for delivery. Prices subject to change without notice.

A spectacular new fantasy adventure series from
America's #1 series publisher!

ROSS ANTON COE #1

WARRIOR OF VENGEANCE

SORCERER'S BLOOD

In the epic sword and sorcery
tradition of the mighty Conan, here
is the blood-laden new
adventure series about a pre-medieval
warrior who confronts wild boars,
monstrous eelsharks, man-eating centipedes,
mind-controlled zombies, murderous
raiders, vengeful allies… and the
greatest wizard of them all — Talmon Khash.

☐ 41-709-8 WARRIOR OF VENGEANCE #1: $2.25
Sorcerer's Blood

Buy them at your local bookstore or use this handy coupon
Clip and mail this page with your order

───

⊙ **PINNACLE BOOKS, INC.** — Reader Service Dept.
1430 Broadway, New York, NY 10018

Please send me the book(s) I have checked above. I am enclosing $ _____ (please
add 75¢ to cover postage and handling). Send check or money order only — no cash or
C.O.D.'s.

Mr. / Mrs. / Miss _____

Address _____

City _____ State / Zip _____
Please allow six weeks for delivery. Prices subject to change without notice.